THROUGH PELICAN EYES

THE FIRST JESSIE MURPHY MYSTERY

jd daniels

D1568924

SAVVY PRESS

NEW YORK

For information address: Savvy Press http://www.savvypress.com

ISBN 978-1-939113-24-5
Library of Congress Control Number:
2014930085

Cover Art by Peg Cullen
Book Design by Carrie Spencer

Printed in the United States of America

SAVVY PRESS-GAWANUS BOOKS-SAGE SF PUBLISHERS
Distributed Worldwide
FIRST EDITION

It will be found, in fact, that the ingenious
are always fanciful, and the truly imaginative
never otherwise than analytic.
~ Edgar Allan Poe

The author wishes to acknowledge the
invaluable assistance of the following people:
Ellen Larsen, Marjorie Carlson Davis, Claudia Bischoff,
Suzanne Kelsey, Marsha Perlman, Jeannette
Batko, Sandy Daniels and editor, Elizabeth Ann Tyson. She
would also like to thank her family, Tom
and her
Matlacha neighbor Stokely Moore
for their encouragement and shared laughs
during the writing process. And last but not least,
she gives special thanks to Peg Cullen, the award-winning
artist who painted the cover.

Prologue

Okay, so I shouldn't be doing this. I mean, he doesn't know I'm coming. I didn't even tell my friends in Cambridge that I was leaving, except the guy who I hired to look after the rentals. It's ridiculous, really—me, doing this.

My name is Jessie Murphy. I'm a half Irish/half English property manager, a wannabe "I really don't have any time to create" artist, and my last job was with a really hot P.I. named Hawk. My best bud is a plaster of Paris gargoyle and I'm not ashamed to say that I talk to him. Will Rolins is my guy. He lives on a trust fund, is smart, obsessive and currently focused on hunting for buried treasure. He left for Florida a month ago. I begged off the trip. I mean, you can only follow a guy around so many times, right?

I'm absolutely sure he's horny by now. Absolutely positive. No question about it.

Now, don't get me wrong, it's not that I think he'd have sex with another gal. Not Will. He's honest as a new born. Besides, he knows I'd never, never forgive him if he had sex with another girl while we were still in a relationship. I mean, ewww.

There just comes a time when a girl has to follow her wild side. It's not that *I'm* horny. No way.

Since starting the long drive, I've been focusing on my most vivid memory of Will. He's naked and standing on a distant boulder facing the sea. It's July and I'm twenty-three. It's my first time at a nude beach and I'm hesitant to take off my bathing suit. But I pull down my bikini straps and smile as Will raises his arms and dives, skimming the water like a low-flying pelican.

Will, babe, hang on tight—Jessie is comin`!

1

The purpose of art is not a rarefied, intellectual distillate—it is
life, intensified, brilliant life.
                                                              ~ Alain Arias-Misson

"Oh, Gar, I can't wait to see his face." I chuckled as we
passed a giant blow-up snowman swaying between two palms.

Music filled the car's interior. I tapped to the beat on the
steering wheel as I swung left on May Street and slid into a
gravel driveway. Frowning I eyed crime scene tape stretched
over one of the duplex's front doors.

"Whoa, looks like there's trouble in par…ee…dise." I
stepped out of the car and patted all available pockets,
searching for the slip of paper I had written Will's address on.
I crinkled my nose. The gas station. The toilet I wouldn't sit
on. Darn.

I racked my memory. Number 12. Had to be 12. The tape
was on door 10. Yep—12. Good. "Come on. Will can fill us
in." I unstrapped Gar and holding him under my left arm,
smiled. "Okay, shhh, we want to surprise him, quiet." I tiptoed
toward the one-story cement block building. Knocked.
Nothing. Knocked louder.

"Yoohoo…Will!"

"Go away, we don't want any!"

I grimaced. Sounded like my Grandma Murphy on a good day. "Will! It's Jessie!" Turning my back to the tape on the other door, I tightened my grip on Gar and waited.

The door swung inward. A sleepy-eyed, really, really long-haired blonde woman glared at me. Her expression went from irritation to sad in a blink of her false eyelashes. "Oh, dear…it's you."

I didn't know this woman anymore than I knew the species of palm tree that had just dropped a dead frond longer than my body on the hood of my car. Probably a king, I figured. A queen wouldn't be so rude. Granted my car is old, but really. The woman seemed confused and reminded me of a mermaid, what with her gold sequined pants and parrot green tank top that showed her more than generous suntanned girls to high advantage. The cigarette in her right hand was a nice touch too. Had Will gotten word that I was coming and as a joke invited this woman over to greet me?

"Hon, you come on in. Excuse the mess. It doesn't sound like you've heard."

"Heard what?" Expecting Will to pop out and yell surprise, I craned my neck. The place smacked of hurricane damage. A putrid stench of mold assaulted my nostrils. I didn't step inside.

She apparently assumed I was entering, because she said, "I'll get you a glass of water."

Water out of the tap? Was this sea nymph kiddin'? I don't think so.

"What haven't I heard?"

"Why, about…" She jerked her head to the left, indicating the other side of the duplex. "That poor fella—your guy, hon. He showed me your picture. I'm real sorry to have to tell you this, but he was found, oh dear, there's no easy way to say this—dead. They say he killed himself."

Okay, so I'd play along with this. I mean, as a woman with a plaster of Paris bud, what could I expect? People were always trying to pull one over on me. With a dramatic sweep of my arm, I placed my hand over my heart. "Oh my God! No. It's not possible. It can't be." I made my shoulders slump. *Revenge is sweet, Will. Just you wait.*

"Oh, honey, I'm so sorry."

Like, enough, right? I couldn't keep my eyes from narrowing. "How did he...uh, do it?"

I thought of asking if it were by an overdose of dark chocolate, but I didn't want to give the woman the pleasure of laughter.

"I guess, well, I guess he done shot himself."

I gazed at her in mock horror. "Shot himself? You mean with a gun?" I lowered my head to hide my curling lips. *Will with a gun? Hardly.* Her toenails were decorated with starfish. I glanced at her fingernails, seashells. *How quaint.* Swallowing my smile, I raised my head higher.

The woman must have suspected I thought this was a joke, because she was examining me as if I had two heads. She hurried away and returned with a newspaper clipping. The photo was Will. I read the headline. My heart felt like someone had blown air into it and it was in danger of exploding. A tightly drawn rubber band of horror snapped at me. Wild-eyed, gasping for breath, I grabbed for the doorframe. The paper fell to the terrazzo floor. I moaned and collapsed.

Two hours later with swollen eyes and shaking hands I parked in front of the green and white, one-story government building holding the Lee County Florida Sheriff's Office in Fort Myers on Six Mile Cypress. A white pelican landed on the flag pole and gazed down at me. Will's personal totem was the white pelican. I rested my head on the back of the car seat, my attention on the bird—inhaling—exhaling—refusing to believe, until straightening my shoulders, I leaned over and released Gar from his seatbelt.

Chunks of seashells crunched under my flip flops like potato chips in a bag. The blacktop, heated by the late afternoon sun, gave off a petroleum smell. A series of sharp whistles made me shudder. I made out a white body and streaked brown breast at the top of a parking lot light.

I entered the building, slid my sunglasses over my tan cap and introduced myself to the uniformed dispatcher who sat at a metal desk behind a glass window. Portraits of George Washington and Barack Obama hung on the cream-colored wall. A calendar with an imposing pileated woodpecker feeding on the trunk of a palm reminded me it was December 26th, my deceased mother's birthday.

Gazing steadily at my puffy eyes, then at Gar, with skepticism written all over her face, the perfume-doused dispatcher came out of her enclosed room, holding a scanner. "I'll have to check that." She pointed at Gar. "Set it on the floor."

Like a blank-faced robot I followed her orders. When she was through scanning Gar, she eyed me again, asked me to raise my arms and ran the machine along my body.

"The sheriff's office is through that door, third one on the left. I'll buzz you in."

I thanked her, picked up Gar and walked the window-less corridor lined with photos of officers in uniform. A tarnished brass door plate was embossed with the words: *Marc Schilling: Sheriff.* I knocked. The haunting sound echoed down the hallway. I stared at the metal nameplate, feeling weightless, disconnected, cut off from my surroundings.

A gruff voice invited me in. Picturing Will's face, I opened the door and was taken aback by a cold blast of air. I stepped forward, but tripped. "Ouch!" I grabbed for the door jamb. Embarrassed, I bent to rub my throbbing, reddened big toe.

The sheriff came to my side. "Are you okay?"

I assured him I was, but I wasn't and it had nothing to do with my stubbed toe. He smiled and extended his hand. I shifted Gar to my other arm. The sheriff wrapped his thick fingers around my palm, glanced at Gar, then at me. Grunting inaudible words, he motioned for me to take a seat. Everything seemed to be in slow motion. I settled into a chair and set Gar on the floor to my right. Nothing was real about this. Nothing.

The oak desk was littered with paperwork. A bronze deer

paperweight held a cigar in its antlers. It sat to the left of the sheriff's imposing upper torso with a machine to his right. His uniform was crisp. A photograph of a woman and two kids hung on the tan wall above his head and was flanked by two plaques.

Perhaps if I concentrated on the picture long enough I would start feeling normal. I swallowed hard and gave my full attention to the teenage girl. I was struck by how much she looked like the sheriff: The same pointed, straight nose, identical curl of the lips and eye shape. I only hoped she didn't have his super-sized wing nut ears. The girl had on a navy blue shirt that matched her dad's. I wondered if she or her parents had intentionally created this resemblance to the sheriff. Except for the fact that his hair was streaked with gray, their hair was the same dark brown.

Focusing worked. I sat up straighter. "Nice family shot."

The sheriff withdrew the cigar from the antlers. He shot another glance toward my eyes and then studied something to the left of my ear.

"Yeah, too bad they've grown up to be such a disappointment. My daughter won't even admit I'm her dad," he said, eyeing me warily. "After our phone conversation, I really thought you wouldn't come. How can I help you?"

I put my hand on Gar's head. "Sheriff, I know your time is valuable, so I'll get right to the point. As you know, I'm here about the recent suicide in Matlacha."

Schilling made a tower with his fingers.

I dipped my head. "I was wondering if there was any indication, any evidence at all, that the deceased wasn't Will Rolins."

The sheriff eyed Gar, then me.

"We talked about that on the phone. As I told you, Will Rolins was the victim. There was no doubt about that. The case, Ms. Murphy, is closed. The scene was investigated and people who knew Rolins were interviewed. The investigative detective determined that there was no foul play and that the scene was consistent with suicide."

Forcing back tears I placed my elbows on the arms of the chair and pressed down. "It was definitely Will?" My words seemed unreal to me.

"Absolutely. It was his sister who identified him in the morgue. Poor dear, she was so distraught."

I glanced back at the portrait. After several seconds I asked, "Is there any way I can read the police report?"

His facial expression tightened ever so slightly. "Our police reports are not public, Ms. Murphy."

I was speechless. This was a bold-faced lie. My red flag of warning shot up the pole.

"It's always hard to understand when a loved one, well, does what he did." Schilling readjusted his broad shoulders in the black leather arm chair. His tone was mellow and controlled. "But, my dear, I assure you, your friend Will Rolins shot himself." With the last words, beads of sweat popped out on his forehead. He touched a button on the machine on his desk. "Mary, turn up the damn air-conditioning."

"But in the last letter I received from him there was absolutely no indication he was depressed."

The sheriff replaced the unlit cigar across the deer antlers. "These things are hard to figure out. I had a school chum who called all his old buddies, including me, and invited us to go hunting on his place." He swiped his forehead. "It was as if he were taking care of us, wanting his pals to get together again. He killed himself the day before we arrived. It was a shocker." He cleared his throat. "One never knows. What I can tell you, is this: The man we found definitely ended his own life. It wasn't a pretty sight. You don't need the gory details, but there is no doubt at all about the cause of Will Rolins` death. He shot himself." He wiped his brow again. "This heat is killin` me!"

"Can I see the…" Oh, am I really asking this? "the body."

He looked at my hands. "I'm sorry my dear. His sister had him cremated. Under the circumstances, I couldn't blame her." His eyebrows furrowed. "Didn't she phone you?"

Blood rushed from my head. Cremated? I would never see Will again? I was unable to suppress a moan.

"Oh dear, you mean you didn't hear about this until now? Goodness, I'm so sorry." He shuffled uncomfortably in his seat.

I raised my hand to fend off more sympathy and closed my eyes. A motor kicked in. The room's temperature dropped two more degrees, while with my hand over my mouth, I fought for control.

When I dared to open my eyes again, the sheriff was writing. With a quiver in my voice, I thanked him, apologizing for questioning his authority.

"That's all right, my dear. You're in shock. I understand."

Fearing the sheriff was going to lean over the desk and pat me on my tan cap, I stood and picking up Gar, backed toward the door. "Thanks so much for your time. You've been very kind." I had to get out of there before…before….I just had to get out of there…I rushed outside.

Opening the car door, I strapped in Gar and then slid in behind the steering wheel. My hand shook as I reached for the stick shift. It can't be. It just can't be.

I reversed, then pulled over to the curb and drew my iPhone from my breast pocket and clicked on a contact.

"Hey!"

"Jessie, is that you? Where the hell are you? I'm standing at the foot of your steps. They're covered in snow."

"I'm in Florida."

"What?"

"I, uh, changed my mind and decided to join…" I paused before saying, "Will."

"Ah, well, cool. I'm sure that has made him a very happy man. Did you take your art tools?"

It took me several seconds to answer. "Hawk."

"Why the tone of doom and gloom? Are you regretting the decision already?"

I couldn't help myself, I broke down and sobbed.

"Jessie! Jesus. What's wrong?"

Between gasps, I told Hawk the news.

"My, God. Listen, I'll come down there to get you. You

can't drive back by yourself. Holy Christ."

I cleared my throat. "No. I'm not coming back yet."

"Are they having the funeral down there? Surely his…"

I interrupted him. "Hawk, Will didn't kill himself, not with a gun."

"Jessie, please! You do know you're in mourning, don't you? People don't make wise decisions after getting such a shock. Don't think you can get involved with this. Leave it up to the cops. He had problems with depression. You've always known that."

"I can't leave, not yet. I got a letter from Will the day he died. He asked me to come help him dig. He was excited, not depressed. It only took the letter two days to get to me. Even if he went off his medication, it would have taken longer than that for him to go that low. The facts don't add up. He was murdered."

"Good, God. Murdered?" There was a long pause, and then he said: "Okay, okay. I know how stubborn you are. What is it you need?"

"Right now I just have one question."

"Sure, what?"

"I want a copy of the police report. How do I get it? I know it's possible."

He sighed. "It's simple, just file a FOIA. That's a Freedom of Information Act request. You can do it online. But be sure and make up some good excuse for requesting the report or you won't get it."

"That's all? By the way, the sheriff told me they weren't public. Seems odd, don't you think?"

"Ah, you know how it is, some people in power like others to think their world is so important the rest of the world can't be privy to it. Don't jump to conclusions. I'll order this for you. That's the least I can do. I'll call you once I get it. And Jessie, I am so, so sorry." After waiting for my reply which I didn't give he said goodbye and the phone went dead.

I kept it in my palm until I heard my laughing monkey ringtone.

"You remember the core rule right? Never, never face a suspected killer alone with your suspicions."

"How could I forget, it's your mantra."

"Well, you make it yours too. Promise?"

"Sure."

And Jessie, I am so very sorry for…for…this..." Hawk disconnected again and with a trembling hand I pocketed my phone.

I stared into space. Will was dead. What should I do?

"Find his killer." The words came in the voice of my feisty Irish Grandma Murphy. I put my hand on my forehead, closed my eyes and wept.

I should have come with him. This would never have happened if…

"Action, Jessie. Use the brain that God gave you. That's the only answer for grief."

Okay, Grandma. Okay.

Tonight I'd force myself to use Will's letters to create a list of people to question. It didn't take me long to decide that I'd present myself as the grieving girlfriend trying to gather information to help me understand why Will killed himself. People would be less guarded if they didn't know they were potential suspects.

"So, Gar, what if I find out I'm wrong?"

But Gar was the silent type. He said nothing.

Looking straight ahead, I pressed down on the gas pedal and drove away, letting the tears flow.

The motel I checked into on West Island, like many of the other commercial buildings, was painted royal blue, red and yellow. The one-story building was surrounded by Matlacha Pass on three sides. A wrap-around dock was fitted with Adirondack chairs painted in brilliant yellow, green, purple, and blue. Each chair back had been sawn into a fish shape.

My efficiency was the farthest one from the county road and included a small refrigerator and a hotplate. I had only one suitcase and a cooler to unpack; it wasn't like I'd planned to spend the winter months.

Emptying the thawed ice from the cooler into the sink, I sat three Guinness bottles and a carton of water in the refrigerator and positioned the cooler upright to dry. My clothes fitted into the dresser with room to spare. To keep out all things evil, I placed Gar on the nightstand facing the door. It took no more than ten minutes to be at home. Now, to the business at hand, finding the killer without anyone knowing I was investigating.

I unscrewed the top off a bottle of water, took a long drink and picked up the first letter I'd received from Will. Like a burrowing owl entering her underground den, I sunk into two overstuffed pillows and read the salutation, *Dear Weiner*. I stopped and looked up at the ceiling, blinking fast, then read it again. I skimmed over a description of a sculptor named Jay Mann, and some unnamed woman who reminded Will of me that he said I should meet.

"Listen to this, Gar: *I've signed several documents with property owners getting permission to search their land. Bokeelia, at the northern tip of Pine Island, is where Bru Baker, the famous pirate I told you about, lived. This is the time, Weiner, I can taste success.* He could always taste success, couldn't he?

"So, please, little stubborn one, come to the islands with Gar. He'll bring me luck. It will be good for you. Find someone else to manage those apartments for a month. Put down your plumbing tools and pack your paints and canvas. This place is an artist's dream come true. I miss you. You can paint to your heart's desire and in your spare time be my digging partner. Just imagine what it would be like to pull a chest out of the sand, dust it off, open it, and see GOLD coins that haven't been touched for centuries!! Think of what the historic society would say when we presented it to them? You could paint a picture of our find and we'd hang it over the couch—our couch—the one with all the stains. Much love, Your Butternut. Okay, I won't cry. I won't."

I stood and began to pace the small room. "So, let's see. He found treasure and someone killed him for it. Someone smart enough to make the crime scene pass as a suicide." I swirled on Gar. "Possible, right? I know, I know, I need to prove it, but it's a darn sound theory." I crossed the room two more times, stopping again in front of Gar. "Yes, I know, I should never have let him come here alone. If I'd been with him, I could have watched his gullible, too-easy-to-be-fooled back. You don't need to remind me."

The letter was dated November 10th, one week after his arrival on the island. What had happened after that? I folded the letter and slipped it back into the envelope. "Okay, I need a plan."

Making plans was one of my weaker traits. I preferred to fly by the seat of my tattered, thrift store jeans, but circumstances dictated actions. A plan it would be. First, I needed to find out what Will's time in Matlacha was like.

I finished off a Guinness before pulling the cellophane from a stack of four by six note cards. On the first one I wrote: People to talk to. The list was short and dictated by the letter: 1. Jay Mann, the sculptor. 2. The unnamed woman. 3. Unknown property owners. 4. Others who knew Will.

Chewing on the pencil eraser I pondered, then wrote on another card: 1. Ask around the local watering hole, Bert's, about Will, his friends, what they know about him and the day he died. 2. Go to Will's apartment to search for the papers he signed with property owners, his log and map. 3. Talk to his neighbors 4. Talk with Jay Mann, the sculptor.

I glanced down at Gar. "Stop looking at me!" I switched off the light and hugging a pillow curled into a fetal position.

"Like, I'm not perfect. Okay?

2

*The painter and the canvas are alone, and if the canvas does
not fight back, it is meaningless.*
~ Edward Millman

At 10 a.m. I sat up with the abruptness of a startled
cormorant and yanked back the blue sheet. But then I
remembered where I was, and what had happened and that I
didn't have an early morning schedule to keep. I nestled back
into the pillow and allowed sorrow to wash over me until, like
a scolding mother, the roar of the nearby highway commanded
me to rise and shine. I shuffled to the window and opened the
blinds. A white egret stood on the dock staring out over the
water. I pulled up the window pane and inhaled the salty scent
of the sea. The egret spread its wings, retracted its neck and
with a croaking cuk cuk cuk flew away with the speed of a
rising hot air balloon. I breathed in and out, taking in the sense
of peace the sea offered, but was unable to receive.

Running my tongue around the inside of my mouth, I riled
up the taste of hours-old beer and headed for the bathroom.

I didn't shower, but I brushed my teeth, then pulled on my
undies, favorite blue shorts, a gray Lycra sleeveless shirt, white

socks, walking shoes and my lucky tan cap. I'm the kind of person who is proud I paid no more than a dollar for any item, except for the socks and shoes and panties, of course. One has to be discriminating about what items of used clothing they'll wear. Tying a fifty-cent sweatshirt from Goodwill around my waist, I left the motel to start my day, as I began every day, with an arm-pumping, sweat-producing power walk. I'd tried running when I was a teen, but it hurt my knees.

In long strides I passed by a conglomeration of pastel brightly painted galleries, craft shops, restaurants, boats of all varieties, shack-sized houses, and million dollar homes situated on canals. When the area was first settled, it had been dubbed Mat-la-`shay, possibly a name meaning "water to the chin" given by the original inhabitants, the Calusa Indians. With four-hundred plus homes and a busy, narrow street and a drawbridge that cut the town in two, it was a place easy to pass through.

But two years before when Will and I had spent a week on the island, we found it difficult to leave. My shoulders slumped. My pace slowed. It was no surprise to me that it was here that Will had rented half of a duplex while he searched the nearby Pine Island with his metal detector. Will was a sucker for romance and he loved diversity. Ah, Will.

I shook off the overpowering sadness as sweat dripped down my forehead and into my eyes. Weaving through parked trucks and cars, I headed back to the room to shower.

Seconds before noon I entered the dark interior of Bert's Bar & Grill with my sketch pad and drawing pencil. As my eyes adjusted to the change in light, I nodded at the bartender. The crowded room had a pool table, TV and a wrap-around bar. Every stool was filled. I pushed back memories of my times with Will here and slipped by three people chatting with a waitress near the cash register.

The ceiling of the room I settled in had dark-green rafters. The walls were painted a deep enamel blue. License plates from numerous states were tacked to cross beams. The floor was painted black. A mural of mangrove islands filled one corner near a mounted giant marlin. Another corner was the home of a pair of Yamaha speakers and a mike. The place buzzed with laughter and conversation.

I gazed into the vacant sockets of a steer skull that seemed to be looking as intently back at me. Unlike Georgia O'Keeffe, not being inspired by animals that had long ago given up their flesh, I averted my eyes and faced the much more appealing view of the bay. Two small boats were anchored near the oval "Bert's Bar & Grill" sign that I remembered from our vacation photos. The occupants of the boats were fishing. I turned my attention to the yellow and red French doors with a handle on both sides and my eyes glistened. Will had taken a picture of me in front of those doors.

Crinkling my freckled nose I began to draw Will's face.

"What can I get you, hon?" a waitress asked as she looked at my drawing.

My hand flew up to hide the picture, but before it was covered, she said, "Hey that looks just like..." The waitress frowned, and then addressed me. "What brought you to these parts? Her right incisor was missing. Her smile was broad. Her hair was spiked and dyed carrot red. Rose Thompson. Will's description was right on.

I inhaled. "My, uh, boyfriend died here recently."

Before I could get anything else out of my mouth, Rose raised her voice, "Oh, dear. Really? Why, you're… Hey, Lil, come over here. This is that gal Will talked about. She's sitting right here drawing him." She nodded toward the sketch. "That's good, hon."

My fingers quivered. "Thanks."

"It isn't too healthy sitting all alone drawing the face of someone who's just died." She sat across from me. "Will used to come in here all the time. We were so sorry to hear about his…death."

Another woman leaned on the door frame between the rooms wiping her hands on a towel. She had teased bangs. Her braided, waist-length hair was gray and streaked with white strands. She had high cheekbones and small ears. A pair of rhinestone sunglasses sat high on her head. Her knuckles were swollen. She wore what I assumed was a fake diamond on her left index finger and six earrings in her left ear. She was the bartender that I'd nodded at when I came in.

A limp was obvious as she came to the table. "Your name is Jessie, right? I'm Lil Flowers."

"Yeah."

We shook hands.

Lil took in my body, the sketch, my face and my cap with one swift glance.

More customers walked in.

Rose stood, grabbed two empty beer bottles from a recently deserted table and spoke fast. "You know, Luke Abbot…" She interrupted herself, looking at me. "Have you met him yet?"

I shook my head. "No. I've just arrived." I hadn't met Luke, but I knew from Will's letters that he owned an art gallery in Matlacha. I had no intention of telling people what I knew or didn't know. Not at this point.

"Will told us you were an artist." Rose motioned to the customers who had just sat, and then checked out my drawing again. "Luke owns one of the local galleries. He'll be interested in meeting you."

Lil added, "When Will showed up and decided to hang around, well, we took to him."

"We were hit hard by his…." Rose's voice trailed off.

Lil reached over and touched Rose's arm.

Rose sighed and patted Lil's fingers. "God bless you," she said softly to Lil before turning to me. "The last time I saw him he came in and sat at the bar, staring at a pill bottle."

Someone called Lil's name. She rushed away.

I figured my eyes appeared as if they were going to pop out of my head. I was shocked. I couldn't imagine Will taking his pill bottle anywhere. "He brought his medication into the bar?"

Rose nodded. "Yep. I asked him if they were anti-depressants. I don't know why I thought they were, but I did." She focused on the sketch, apparently remembering. "He didn't say a word. I thought I was talking to a mummy."

A man in a cowboy hat waved for service. "Be right there," Rose called.

"He might have been meditating."

"Meditating? Now why would anyone want to meditate in this place or any place for that matter? Now, praying, that makes sense." Rose walked over to the table and took their order. She gave me a "just a sec" wave and headed for the bar.

As a recovering Catholic I'm not sold on organized religion. Oh, I believe in God, but called him The Universe, as did Will. I did intentions, as did Will. But neither of us actually prayed. But doing intentions, I suppose, is much like praying. I think so, anyway.

A woman in the adjoining room hit a pool ball into a pocket, yelled and did a jig. Her biker companion chased her into the room I was in, pulled her tight and planted a kiss on the iris tattoo on her neck. "You're a beautiful chinchilla."

Rose delivered a pitcher of beer and two glasses and returned to my table. "See what I mean?"

I grinned, but the grin was short-lived. "Yeah, I see, but all the same. Will was known to meditate anywhere."

Rose frowned. "He sure was silent and he didn't move a stitch. If he was meditating he was doing a good job." She tossed another impatient customer a look that said she would be with him in a minute. "I got tired of talking to a seawall so I left him alone. Afterward, I spoke to Lil. We thought he must have been trying to make some decision about those pills."

Lil returned, folded her arms over her chest and spread her legs wide. "Something was wrong. We could tell that. We agreed he needed a talking to. We planned to do it the next time he came in, but we never saw him again."

Lil and Rose shared a grim glance.

"I hoped to get him to come to my church," Rose said. "That man needed to find Jesus."

Will finding Jesus. Under different circumstances that

would be a comical thought. Rose had not been the only one to attempt to convert Will to Christianity. His sister, who he nicknamed the Wicked Witch of the North, had spent years working on him. Will was too broadminded to accept any one faith as the right and only one.

A line of customers was forming. Lil and Rose headed their way.

I picked up my sketch pad and left the bar through the back door. Walking toward the bridge, I stopped at the sight of a lone white pelican preening himself on a piling.

My eyes moistened.

3

*My brushwork is quite unsystematic. I slam the paint on in all
sorts of ways and leave each result to take care of itself.*
~ *Vincent Willem van Gogh*

The following morning after my walk, I arrived at the front
of Will's Matlacha home holding Gar. I didn't want to go into
the rooms where Will had spent his last days, but I knew I had
to.

Two garbage cans sat under the window. A three-inch
lizard, an anole, scurried up one side and disappeared into the
empty interior. Cradling Gar in my left arm, I took the key out
of my pocket and slipped it into the keyhole. The door opened
with a squeak but caught on a rag rug. I wiggled the stubborn
thing until I could shove it the rest of the way open and kicked
the rug to the side. The smell of death made me gasp. I
scanned the room and my heart was sideswiped as my gaze
landed on a two-foot tall fake Christmas tree in a corner.

I bit down on my lip as the image of Will wrapped in
Christmas tree lights playing the role of Light Man came to
mind. I'll never forget how concerned I'd felt when he yelled
for me to plug in the cord. All I could think about was I'd
electrocute him. But he had insisted it was safe, so I plugged

him in. He lit up and began waving his arms and dancing around the yard. Will, my Light Man; the light of my life.

Gathering my Irish wits about me I placed Gar to the right of the entrance near a mop and a broom. "Don't let anyone in." I slid the bill of my cap higher on my head.

I went first to the jalousie kitchen window, cranked it open and stood at the sink for several seconds taking in the fresh air. An animal must have died in here and not been taken out, perhaps a mouse. Walking around the apartment that was smaller than any I managed up north, I stopped in front of the desk where the odor was the most pungent. I slid the heavy wooden piece of furniture across the stained shag carpet and jumped back with a cat-like cry. Picking up a discarded newspaper, I averted my eyes. I hunkered down, felt for the rat's tail, and holding the foul thing at arm's length, carried it to the garbage can outside. Then I scrubbed my hands at the sink with dish soap, wiped them on my shirt and began my search.

No map graced any of the walls. I inspected the area above the desk and found four holes obviously made from tacks where the map most likely had been. Pulling open the desk's one drawer, I found only scraps of blank paper. I rifled through closets, nightstand drawers, cabinets, raised pillows and the mattress, scoured every possible hiding place, but found no log or map or signed permission papers. The cops must have taken them.

A cockroach with the shape of a lima bean, but far uglier and almost as fat as a sumo wrestler, ran out from under a stack of unwashed laundry. I cringed. "Ewww."

Stepping outside I withdrew my cell from my breast pocket and phoned the sheriff's office. Luckily, he was in and answered. Apparently, the female dispatcher was out.

"Hello, Sheriff, this is Jessie Murphy. I forgot to ask if you knew if there was a map and log taken from the apartment."

"Why do you want to know that?"

Watch it, girl. "I was hoping to find a log or a map as a keepsake. I'm making a scrapbook of Will's time in

Matlacha," I said. "You or the investigative team didn't find anything like a log, did you?"

"Oh! Scrapbooking! My wife is a scrap booker too. Well, I wish I could help you with this, but I don't recall that these items were found."

"Okay, thanks anyway." So the killer took them. Not evidence admissible in court, but enough to confirm my belief in the cause of Will's death.

"I assume you'll be heading back north soon?" the sheriff asked.

I thought fast. "Well, to tell you the truth, Sheriff, I just might hang around a bit. I'd forgotten how soothing the sea is."

"Oh, well, you take care. Our Florida sunshine certainly can help the grieving process."

Satisfied that my cover wasn't blown, I thanked him once more and pocketed my phone, then pulled it out again and clicked on a contact. "Hello, Millie, this is Jessie Murphy."

"What do *you* want?"

No, hi, how are you doing, so nice to hear from you. Oh, no. Just a demanding question, Will's sister's style.

"I'm in Matlacha. In fact, I'm standing outside of Will's apartment. I was wondering if you took anything out of it."

"Good God! What are you asking? Do you really think *I* would touch things in that filthy, dreadful place? Why, it…it…!" Without finishing the sentence the phone went dead.

Witch.

Like always, after talking to Will's sister I felt dirty. The woman hadn't even told me about her brother's death. And she had had Will cremated. Oh, God! To Millie, I was a bad chapter in her brother's life. There was a reason Will wanted nothing to do with her. The woman was low on soul.

Discouraged, I returned inside and went into the bathroom. As expected, all of his personal items were missing. I went to another window, opened it and saw what appeared to be an abandoned boat tied to the dock. A white pelican soared across the bow. I headed outside.

I did a thorough search of the exterior of the boat, including the folds of the sail, but found nothing. A padlock secured the cabin. I inspected the mechanism. It was corroded and had no marks that made me think it had been disturbed in years.

A crisp snapping noise startled me. I froze. Another snap told me that someone was near. The hair on the back of my neck tingled. Prepared to greet the visitor and explain why I was on a boat that neither I nor Will owned, I straightened and turned.

A flash of bare leg vanished. I called out, but no one answered or appeared from around the building.

Hopping onto the dock, I hurried to the front of the duplex and knocked on the door of the other half. The woman who told me of Will's death answered, holding a black coffee mug. "Yeah." She opened the door only a crack. "Oh, it's you. Come on in." She walked to a round iron table and chair set. "Come sit."

The living room was furnished with a bamboo sofa and two chairs. The cushions were orange and were made out of a tough fabric that had stained through the years. A hole had been sawn out of one wall for an air-conditioner. Two windows were covered with vinyl blinds. The mildew smell was replaced by one of bleach.

She told me her name was Les and offered me a cup of coffee, which I declined. "My fella's sleeping. How can I help you?"

"I was wondering if you were home the night of Will's death."

"Nah, sorry we weren't, we were fishing on the bridge." The woman's skin was the color of a leather handbag. She stirred her coffee with a plastic spoon.

"So you didn't hear the, uh, gunshot?"

"Oh, yeah, hon, we did. If you look behind you, you'll see the bridge isn't that far away. We were fishing on this end. Besides, sound travels across water. Oh, we heard the pop all right, but neither of us thought much about it. We hear lots of noises around here."

"You didn't by chance see anyone come out the door or come around the duplex that night, did you?"

"Now, why would we see that? It was a suicide. The papers said so."

I didn't want to tip her off. "Yes, I know, but sometimes people kill themselves in front of another person and that person freaks out and runs."

The woman unfolded her arms and scratched her leg. "Well, maybe, sure, I can see that might happen. But I sure didn't see anyone."

"Did you happen to notice if Will had many... uh, visitors?"

The woman's frown was deep. "Like women friends?"

Ouch. "Or men."

"A couple of times I saw a woman at his door. Once it was after midnight." She sneezed.

"Bless you." I really, really didn't want to hear that there was another woman. "And you didn't know who it was?"

"Can't say that I did."

"Was it the same woman each time?"

"I can't really say, sorry."

I began to stand, then changed my mind and asked another question: "Did you and Will talk much?"

"Ah, no, no more than a hello or nod. Your guy was usually gone before I got up. I work nights."

I motioned toward the closed bedroom door. "How about your friend, did he talk much with Will?"

"You'd have to ask him that. But, as I said, he's indisposed right now. Sorry."

I ended the conversation by leaving my phone number and asking what was the best time of day to catch her friend. Then I knocked on the door of the small house to the left, but no one answered. I did the same to every house on this side of the road and bridge, but no one came to their door. Crossing the street I repeated my knocking with no results. Disappointed, I went back to Will's and retrieved Gar.

I didn't know what I'd expected to find in the apartment. I'd worked for the private eye agency long enough to know that crime scenes were thoroughly cleaned out. Will had been dead little over a week. No matter what the sheriff said, I was positive the case wasn't officially closed. The wheels of the government didn't turn that fast. And telling me that police reports weren't open to the public, what was that all about? Hawk was probably right; the sheriff most likely was one of those people who hated his authority to be questioned.

Back in my motel room, thinking of the vanishing bare leg, I locked the door before picking up Will's third letter. I was relying on the letters to be guides. I had almost pitched them, but something made me drop them in a drawer, then bring them with me. Facing Gar, who I sat under the spotlight of the lamp again, I began to pace the room while reading. Two names popped out: Judge and Mrs. Lakewood.

A boat horn sounded. I took out two more cards and wrote the name Lakewood on the top line. Not finding them listed in the phone book, I decided would soon drive to Pine Island Center and use the public computers at the library to find out where they lived.

I picked up Jay Mann's card and tapped it on my palm. It was time to meet the sculptor to find out what he knew about Will's time on the islands.

4

I paint and sculpt to get a grip on reality…
to protect myself.

~ Alberto Giacometti

Going through the white picket gate in front of the house Will had described so aptly, I reminded myself that any person I met was a potential suspect. I repositioned my cap over my freshly washed hair and whispered, "So watch your butt, girl."

A deeply tanned man with a scar across his nose, a thick neck and a shaved head opened the door. He wore no shirt, had a hairless broad chest and his jean shorts had more holes in them than a block of Swiss cheese. He seemed to be pushing forty. His muscular right bicep was tattooed with a snake with its mouth open. I hesitated. This skinhead or aging weight lifter was a friend of Will's? Really? Afraid I'd come to the wrong house again, I introduced myself as Will Rolins` girlfriend and told him I was looking for Jay Mann, the sculptor.

He glanced over his shoulder, then seeming to have made his decision, stepped to the side. "Come in," he said in a solemn tone. "You must be feeling like shit."

The room smelled of burnt lawn clippings. Pot. When he

moved to the side, I caught my breath in amazement. Back-dropped by the view of sky, sea and mangrove islands I was surrounded by a sculptor's studio and art. The west wall was filled floor to ceiling with chisels, carving sets, rifflers, files and rasps. The beige east wall was lined in plaster plaques above various figures on elongated bases positioned on a cube-shaped counter. A chart of the human muscular system leaned against an easel. A life-sized sculpture of what had to be the poet and songwriter Bob Dylan stood just right of the center of the room. The original clay and smaller plaster model sat on a nearby table. A sculpture of a manatee with baby filled one corner. Another life-sized sculpture of a woman with arm over her head in a dancer pose stood in a corner. Galvanized buckets and a crumpled plastic tarp hid one leg of a worktable. A bank of skylights let in light. "Wow, I see why Will was impressed!" I moved on, stopping at a table strewn with what appeared to be pieces of eight. "These seem really old."

"Ah, they're nothin`."He lead me through a patio door that hadn't been cleaned in years.

But I knew valuable old coins when I saw them. I'd learned something from Will. I wondered why he dismissed them so quickly as I stepped onto the dock.

Jay motioned for me to sit on a faded blue director's chair and patted the heads of two Rottweilers.

I've always been leery of people who would own a Rottweiler. I know it's not the dog that is naturally mean. It's the owner who trains them that way. Surely, Will wouldn't be friends with a mean guy. But still...

Jay sat on a wooden crab trap and leaned against a piling. A dolphin rose and disappeared. Pelicans plunge-dove while seagulls circled and filled the air with warning. A woman in a kayak paddled toward an island. The sweet aroma of a potted jasmine mingled with the scent of dead organic matter. I looked at the dogs. They looked at me. I wondered if they could smell my fear. Jay asked me how long I'd been in Matlacha. We chatted about my trip before I turned the subject to my purpose. "Will wrote of you in his letters."

"He did? That's a surprise." Jay's lips formed a pencil-thin, tense grin.

Tense? Why tense?

"He said he liked you." I returned my attention to the dogs. I was glad I hadn't brought Gar. It wouldn't be a fair fight.

Jay leaned his back on a piling. "Well, that's good to know. Not everyone around here holds that opinion." He glanced upward. "Did you have anything specific to talk to me about? I have to meet a guy." The dogs raised their heads.

I shot up from the chair. "I'm sorry. I've come at a bad time. I've just arrived and heard…and well, I guess I'm still…in shock. I'm not thinking straight. Coming unannounced was rude of me." I stepped away from the Rottweilers.

Jay's tone softened. "No, no, please, I'm sorry. Please, sit."

The dog's heads lowered, but their eyes remained on my face.

"I have a few minutes. This has to be a difficult time for you. Will apparently gave the impression we were friends, but I'm sorry we really weren't. In fact, I hadn't seen him for weeks until the morning of his death."

I lowered myself in the chair. "Really?"

"Yeah, it was at The Perfect Cup, the coffee house across from the post office." Jay buried his hand in the neck of a dog. The dog's eyes closed momentarily and he seemed to smile.

"I see. Was he alone?"

"Nah, he was talking to Taco, a waitress at Bert's."

Ah, perhaps the unnamed woman mentioned in Will's letters.

"As I'm sure you can imagine it's still hard to believe that he's gone. And, well, I thought if I could talk to people here who knew him, I could better understand why he did what he did."

"I get that. Can't be easy, what you're going through."

"It, uh, isn't." I took a deep breath. "When you saw him

that morning, did he seem down or upset?"

"Now that you ask, he was excited, or seemed to be." He bent forward and ruffled the other dog's ears.

I frowned. "Doesn't that seem like an odd emotion for a man to have on the day he killed himself?" I asked, more to myself than to him.

The dogs' tails flapped on the weathered boards. I felt a zap of alarm sting my heart. I glanced toward the door, calculating.

"I really couldn't say," Jay said.

"Of course not, you didn't know him well." I could be through the sliding glass door in ten steps. But by the second step, I'd be raw meat.

Jay gave me a quick glance. A low rumble came from the throat of both dogs. My eyes rounded.

"They're harmless. Don't worry about them."

Yeah, right.

"When your fella first came to Matlacha, he used to come by the studio. But then he stopped coming around. Don't know why." He stood, as did the dogs. "I'm sorry. I gotta go."

I pushed myself from the chair. "He said the two of you had something in common."

"Well, I suppose we did." With a dog on either side of his body, Jay motioned for me to walk ahead. I would rather have followed, keeping the dogs in my sight, but it was his house.

"Have something in common?" I said over my shoulder.

"My last girlfriend left me to find herself. We had quite a talk about an artist's need for independence and space."

My cheeks reddened. I was glad he couldn't see them. "Yes, well…" My heart stopped thumping as I felt a dog at my side. The dog's head came closer. I gulped, but in no other way could move.

"Jake, leave her alone."

The dog walked away. I opened and closed my icy fingers, making sure they still worked.

"Sorry about that. Jake's a tease. He, like his master, likes women."

Likes women? Is that what that was all about?

Giving Jay a weak smile and asking him if he minded if I talked to him another time, I turned and tried to make it look like I wasn't rushing to the door.

"Hey, wait a sec." Jay scribbled on a piece of paper, then walked over. "Here, this is my phone number. It's best if you give me warning. I'm a busy man."

Safely outside I tugged down the bill of my cap and assured myself that I had over-reacted. Jay Mann was not using the dogs to intimidate me. My reaction was a figment of my imagination and unreasonable fear of Rottweilers. However, the hairs on the base of my neck told me differently. I made a mental note not to meet Jay in his studio again.

I stopped at my motel room to get my sketch pad and pencil and headed for Bert's.

When Lil and Rose saw me they interrupted what they were doing and came to my table. After a few moments of small talk, I told them I was trying to find out what Will had done on his last day. Doing so, I said, might help relieve my pain. They said they were more than happy to help me in any way they could.

"I was told," I said, "that he was seen that morning talking to a waitress from here."

"He was? That's news to me." Rose leaned closer. "Did you get her name?"

"Taco."

Lil made a low growling sound. "Taco? Well, I'm not surprised. That vain girl gets around."

"Does she still work here?"

"Sure. You've probably seen her already. She's the one who spends more time looking in the mirror than at customers."

Rose chuckled.

"She'll be here shortly; if we're lucky, that is. That girl wouldn't know a clock if it up and fell and broke her big toe. She's one ditzy broad. Okay. Okay, buddy, hold your horses." Lil hurried away. So did Rose.

I angled to the back dock and slid onto a bench at a picnic table. Pulling out blank cards from my breast pocket, I added Taco, Rose, Lil and Luke to my list.

A bobbing boat moored in the bay and I remembered another time when Will and I had rented a sailboat and anchored off shore all day, making love, munching on cheese, crackers, grapes and sipping wine. Fingers touched my shoulder. Rose motioned toward the inner room. A young woman set two mugs on a table. She was good looking in a raw, sexy, gypsy sort of way. It had to be the mystery woman of Will's letter. I stood and went inside.

The room vibrated with cracks of pool balls and loud voices. Two players dressed in frayed cut-offs and sleeveless shirts ogled me. I yanked my tan cap lower on my forehead. A sign painted in bold letters read: *Women Love the Simple Things in Life – Men.* I wove my way through four leering guys.

Lil nodded sideways at the waitress, signaling she was Taco. "I told her you were looking for her," she said in a hoarse whisper.

A man who surely had never worn a condom in his life yelled. "Hey, I'm empty over here!"

Lil put a glass in front of him. "There you are, Gator. Make sure you don't bother the tourists. I had a complaint last week." The man with the week-old beard blew his nose into a paper towel and turned his back on Lil.

I high-tailed it over to Taco. She was now behind the bar gazing into a mirror at her reflection, smiling. Her hair was shoulder-length, thick and black. She held a bar towel.

"Are you Taco?" I slid onto a stool.

"Yep, that would be me. What can I get you, hon?"

"Actually if you don't mind, I'm looking for some information." Her breasts bloomed over her shirt like two well-fertilized hydrangeas that would look good in any vase. I could tell she was a full-of-herself type of gal. I wondered what Will thought she and I had in common? Taco was hot sauce. Me? Medium at best.

"Lil said some artist was looking for me. That you?" Taco asked.

"Yes, but I was also Will Rolins` girlfriend."

Taco dropped the cloth. Swiveling, she headed for the opposite end of the counter, leaving me feeling startled and amazed. I had never seen anyone's whole body language and expression change so quickly or completely.

Lil appeared at my side. "What did you say to her?"

"All I said was that I was Will's girlfriend."

"That's all?"

"Yeah."

"Well, let me talk to her." Lil disappeared into the kitchen.

I sat on a seat two down from Rose who was talking to a man with a four-day-old beard in dirty blue jeans. "I've never worn a girdle and I can tell you right now, I never intend to," Rose said.

The man's voice sounded like the continuous rapping of a drum. "I never said you should. Don't get all riled up. I just said that my wife wears one. God, Rose, you take the cake. Don't take things so serious and personal. The other day we was in the mall and they was selling real pretty girdles and I was tempted to buy you one." He leaned closer. "You know I love you best, baby."

Rose shifted away from him, leaning in my direction. "Keep your voice down, Bill."

Lil and Taco, in a far corner, were deep in conversation. I took a sip of my beer and told myself to stop eavesdropping. The man patted Rose's backside. Rose smacked him on the shoulder and said something in a lower voice. I took out the pencil in my pocket and began to draw.

"You all over your mournin` now, baby?" Bill asked.

My ears perked up.

Rose's voice was steady. "Listen here, Bill, that guy was a friend of mine. Understand?"

"Oh, Rose, baby, I thought you were mad at him. I'm in *need,* baby. Can't you see? Give me a bre..ak!"

Mad at him?

Rose's eyes caught mine in the mirror. She blinked once and dropped her gaze. "Go home to your wife, Bill."

"She's freakin` frigid and you know it. She can't compare nothing to you, baby."

Two men at the bar chuckled and raised their mugs.

Lil frowned and walked away from Taco.

Rose stood and took a step away from the guy.

"Get back here," he said, grabbing her left shoulder.

"Bill!" Rose pulled away

His hand tightened.

My back straightened. This was not my business. Still, no man should manhandle a woman.

"Don't walk away while I'm talkin` to ya—you hear?"

I set my pencil down, and prepared to dial 911, reached for my smartphone.

Rose sat again.

Bill dropped his hand. "That's better."

I shuffled on my seat, swiveled and nailed his hazel daggers with my baby greens.

"Mind your own business, girlie," he said with a sneer.

I did not bat my eyes. He stared back, raised his fist and shook it at me.

Lifting my index finger to tap 911 on my phone, I gave Rose a small, reassuring smile in the mirror. Rose blanched and dropped her gaze.

Lil, favoring her left leg, beat me to the punch. She charged over exuding fire. Her eyes were slits. I was glad I wasn't her target. I slid away.

"What's the idea causing all this brouhaha in here? Don't you ever grab Rose again like that or threaten our customers. You got one minute to be out that door." Her eyes bored into Bill.

He glared back, rubbing his grizzled chin.

Lil reached under the bar and came up holding a short ball bat. "Thirty seconds."

Without another word, he stood and melted through the door. I pocketed my phone.

"You didn't have to do that," Rose said.

"Someone has to look out for you, girl." Lil restored her weapon.

I mean, like, was I impressed or what? The woman was a goddess.

"The Lord looks after me!" Rose's fists were clenched.

Lil gave Rose a disgusted look, took a step away from her and stopped in front of me. "Sorry about that. He had no call to be rude to you."

"No problem, Lil, but thanks for getting rid of him. That was really rad."

Lil chuckled.

"What did Taco say?"

Lil reached for the coffee pot, poured a cup that threatened to overflow, then looked at the bar counter.

"Well?"

"She doesn't like you," Lil said, avoiding my eyes.

"Tell me something I don't know."

"Give her time," Lil said. "She'll come around."

Rose walked to my side and stood in front of Lil.

Glancing first at Rose, then at Lil, I asked, "Was Taco a close friend of Will's?"

"Oh, hon, now don't you go thinkin` such things," Rose said. "He's dead. No reason to start imagining bad things about him. You were his woman. He wouldn't have two-timed you. He's up with God now. May he rest in peace. Never talk bad about the dead."

"I second that," Lil added.

"What did Bill mean when he said you were mad at Will, Rose?"

Rose scratched her arm and rubbed her right shoulder. "Ah, he was remembering an argument Will and I had over something or other. It was nothin`."

A customer called Rose's name. She hurried away. Lil went behind the bar.

I wished I'd done better with Taco and I wished I had half of Lil's power.

Later, at the motel, I climbed onto the bed and picked up the stack of note cards.

On two separate blank cards, I wrote: Had Will told anyone about his treasure hunting? He said he had found something. But, what? Who had he signed the documents with allowing him to dig on their property in Pine Island? Who hated him so badly they'd kill him?

I took the other cards out of my breast pocket and wrote on Rose Thompson's card: Seeing a married man?? Devout Christian. On Lil`s card: Tough. Protective of Rose. Someone I don't want as an enemy. I picked up Taco's card and added: Instant dislike of me. The woman who reminded him of me? Really? On Jay's card, I wrote: Has old gold coins in his possession. Owns two Rottweilers. Has a dynamite studio and is obviously a real artist. Something ended his friendship with Will. After chewing my pencil's eraser, I underlined "artist."

I placed the cards in a perfect line across the nightstand wondering if the Gulf would be warm enough near shore for manatees. I had an affinity for manatees. Will had always said he had a spiritual connection with pelicans. He hoped when he died he'd reincarnate as one. Remembering this, tears threatened to spill.

Focusing on Gar under the harsh light bulb, I slid out of bed, picked up my sunglasses and positioned them over his ears. "Better to hide your staring eyes."

I cocked my head to the right. What was that noise? I tiptoed to the window and raised a blind a fraction of an inch. I couldn't see anyone. There, it happened again. Someone was out on the deck. I grabbed the cold metal handle and then pulled away.

Leaning back against the wall, I listened until I was sure whoever had been walking close to my door was no longer there. I scratched the base of my hairline as my heart pounded. Intuition told me it was someone up to mischief. I have the kind of intuition that sometimes makes you think you know what people are feeling and thinking without even talking to them, the kind that makes some people think you're psychic, although you know you're not.

My arms encircled my T-shirt. No matter how much I attempted to convince myself that it was a harmless passerby, I knew it was someone with sinister intent. My hairline never lied. But I couldn't call the cops. They'd laugh at me.

I scooped up Gar, dove into bed and pulled the comforter up to my chin.

5

I'm afraid if you look at a thing too long,
it loses its meaning.

~ *Andy Warhol*

At noon the following day in Bert's, I watched a woman in a halter top and skin-tight shorts insert a dollar bill into the slot of the jukebox, study the selections and then put her finger on the touch screen. Johnny Cash's sorrowful voice filled the room. The woman, arms high over her head, began to dance.

A man waved a mug. "Hey, Lil, give me another beer, will you?"

Lil crinkled her nose at him. "Yeah. Yeah. Yeah."

Rose was chatting in a loud voice to a female customer. Rose's red hair was pinned behind her ears with two barrettes embossed with the word "Jesus". "Last month I went to Cape Coral and bought a sports bra. It's great to work out in. I've lost five more pounds."

Amused, I shook my head. I'd owned a sports bra once, but couldn't get the thing past my ears without feeling like I was being strangled by Hulk Hogan. Once I got it on I resembled a length of floor board.

Rose continued, "Of course, the woman at the spa said I

had to get rid of my nail polish, because your nails just can't breathe with that stuff on and breathing is important when you exercise."

The customer speaking to Rose giggled and admired her own brightly painted nails. "Is she a Christian?"

"Oh, you bet, hon, I wouldn't go to a spa that wasn't run by a Christian."

Rose strolled to my table and jotted down my order for a bowl of chowder and a tonic and lime, then lingered. I smiled at her. "Hey, Rose, I was wondering if Will ever mentioned he had a hobby."

"You mean his interest in buried treasure?"

I nodded. "Yeah."

"Oh, sure. I've never seen a man more enthusiastic."

"For him, it was all about process."

"I don't doubt that one bit," Rose said.

"Did he ever tell you whose land he was exploring?" I was feeling restless, anxious to move my investigation forward.

"I'd ask Lil about that. I do know he was working steadily. He came in here more than once exhausted from diggin` and sweaty as a day laborer."

"He leaned toward being obsessive." To stop my legs from doing a dance, I propped them up on a chair.

"Oh, yeah." Rose placed one ankle over the other.

"Have you bought a place here?"

"Me? Own a house? Nah, I have sand between my toes. My ancestors were cow-herder Crackers from southern Georgia. I'm a nomad by nature. Heck, I've lived in almost every state up and down the East Coast. I'm not up for any ownership responsibility. Don't even own a car. I can't take any risks like Lil."

"Risks?"

"She bought some land on the northern tip of Pine Island when prices were reaching for the clouds. She almost had to give it back to the bank. She couldn't make the payments."

"Ewww, must have been stressful."

Rose exposed the gap between her teeth. "Oh, yeah. She

was a basket case for weeks, but she's a lucky one. Seems her ex came up with a bundle of cash and she paid off the mortgage. Some women get all the luck. All I got from my ex was a shoebox of unpaid bills."

So Lil owned land in Bokeelia and came into money. Now I'm getting somewhere. "How long ago did she pay off her debt?"

"Two days ago. Can you believe it?"

Rose had just given me a motive for Lil to have killed Will. That is, if I could prove Lil had stolen his find, anyway, after I proved there was a find.

A customer waved his hand for service. Rose, humming *These Boots Are Made For Walkin`,* excused herself and sauntered his way.

I went to the bar where Lil was serving drinks. "Hey, Lil. How's things?"

In reply, Lil waved with her bar towel.

Before Lil was called away again, I quickly asked, "Did you have a chance to talk to Taco?"

"Yeah, and if you're lucky, she'll talk to ya. But be nice. She's still real touchy."

Yeah, like, someone at their first acupuncture visit.

"Okay, thanks. By the way, Rose said you owned land in northern Pine Island. Congrats on paying off the mortgage."

Lil shot a look at Rose that would have stopped a lesser woman in her tracks. But not Rose. She waved gaily and gave her a broad wink. "That woman sure has a big mouth. I don't know why she told you that. But, to tell you the truth, I'm sure glad I took a settlement rather than alimony. That money came in real handy."

I wondered how I could go about confirming Lil's claim. "I guess you knew Will was a treasure hunter?"

"Oh, yeah. He talked to Rose and me about it all the time."

"I don't suppose he was digging on that land you own?"

Lil limped down the bar, took an order and filled it before returning.

"In fact, Will did dig on my land, back in November, but

he didn't find anything. He moved on to another place, but for some reason I could never figure out, he didn't let on where." Without another word, Lil hurried away, passing Taco as she started her shift.

I made a mental note to jot this information down and discuss it with Hawk.

Turning her back momentarily to the customers, Taco faced the mirror, smiled into her reflection, fluffed her hair and then drew a draft.

"Hey, Taco," I said, hoping for a friendlier reaction.

Taco eyed me under her bangs, but did not reply or smile.

"Come on, girl. I just have a few questions. I'm not so bad."

"Yeah, sure. You're the one whose art is more important than those you love, right?"

"Excuse me!"

"Will told me you stayed up north because you needed time alone to paint. Well, that's bull shit! Pure bull shit! I never saw a guy so heartbroken or lonely. Hah! You're a real bitch in my book. You might as well have pulled the trigger yourself! You knew he had a problem with depression!" Taco snapped her chin upward in rebuff.

Shocked at hearing the words I feared were true I lowered my head for several moments. Taco was wrong. She was. When I raised my head, I asked in a hushed voice I was working at keeping steady, "Were you his new girlfriend?"

Taco's eyes narrowed. "Was I his girlfriend? Get real! He was still stuck on you! God, you're thick! He wasn't attracted to me, not the person I am now. It's too bad he killed himself, 'cause in a few weeks, I'll be what he deserved. Course I wouldn't want him then, but well, we'd still be friends."

I swallowed my guilt, but heaps of it stuck in my throat. Will was murdered. He had to have been murdered.

Taco apparently decided she'd said enough. She snapped her mouth shut and began to move down the bar.

I raised my voice. "I heard you and Will had quite a talk the morning he died?"

Taco stopped and turned. "That ain't none of your business." She stomped away.

"Hey! I was talking to you!"

Over her shoulder, Taco gave me the finger.

Disgruntled, I headed toward a table at the water's edge and sat in view of Jay Mann's dock, repeating to myself that Taco was wrong. Rose took my order, delivered my food and left. I wondered what Taco meant when she said that in a few weeks she'd be what Will deserved, but I sure as heck wasn't going to approach her again today. Who needed that headache? Such garbage.

I chewed, hardly noticing when I swallowed. Hearing the door open, I glanced in that direction and watched a couple coming outside. I stopped in mid-chew. It had to be Judge Lakewood and his wife, Esther. Once again, Will's words in his letter were better than a drawing: Expensive clothes, sense of entitlement, uppity demeanor, right height and hair color. And the woman was around fifty-years-old, a high-maintenance knockout. "I couldn't afford her sheets," Will had written.

I waited for them to settle, then picked up my glass and headed to their table. After introducing myself as Will's girlfriend, they asked me to join them. I was all too glad to do so.

As I sat, Esther Lakewood reached out for my hand. Afraid if she touched me I would crumble into a fit of tears, I dropped my hand on my lap. "We're so sorry for your loss," she said in a low, sympathetic voice.

"I...well...thanks." I did not meet her eyes.

"He was a gentle, kind man. Not the type you would expect to die so violently," the judge said.

An awkward silence fell over the table.

"Dolphin!" At the excited yell, the judge and his wife stood and walked to the railing. I stayed where I was. The judge's statement had thrown me into emotional chaos. I began to count from one-hundred backward, a trick I'd learned to make me calm again. By the time the judge and his wife returned, I was composed enough to speak. "I'm sorry. I guess this is all too fresh."

"We understand, my dear. You needn't apologize," the judge said.

I thanked him and asked if he minded if I asked a few questions. They both agreed without reserve.

"You live in Bokeelia?" I knew they did.

"Yes, we have several acres there," the judge said. "Esther would rather live in Matlacha, but I need my privacy. In fact, I'm considering buying an island."

I picked up my glass. "Forgive me if I'm wrong, but didn't Will say that he met you at the Randall Research Center?"

"That's right. Esther and I volunteer there from time to time. He came one day…I think it was on a Saturday, full of questions about the history of the area. We suggested a few books and encouraged him to visit the local museum off Stringfellow Road." He paused, looking at Esther. "I don't believe we saw him again. Did we?"

Esther had been gazing out over the water while her husband talked. At the question, without looking at him, she addressed me. "I saw him another time here. But that's it."

"Oh, really, Esther?" The judge's tone was cold as an ice cube. "When was that?"

Whew! If I were Esther I'd be back peddling. This guy was pissed.

Esther feigned innocence. She rapidly blinked her long eyelashes and said, "Why you remember, silly, when I went to give out business cards around Matlacha. I told you I'd run into him. "

The judge's expression was wooden. Esther smiled again then gazed out to sea.

I wondered if this had satisfied her husband. Jealousy was such a nasty trait. He studied the tabletop for the longest time before addressing me. "My dear," he said, "we *do* wish we could be more helpful. Grieving is such a terrible thing. Have you attended church since his death? God can be a comfort in times like these."

I thanked them again for their concern. The judge invited me to visit them at their home in Bokeelia. Motives for murder like greed and jealousy were rolling around in my head in marquee fashion. I assured him that one day I would contact him and excused myself.

Returning to my table, I blew my nose into a paper towel torn from a wooden holder. I was convinced the Lakewoods were withholding information. I made a note to call them individually and question each of them alone.

I watched Taco serving tables. As she set down a plate she caught the eye of Esther and gave her a curt nod. When Taco saw that I had seen the exchange, she flipped her hair off her shoulder and walked in the opposite direction. Good thing I didn't mind being disliked. Taco's negativity flew right through the glass. I tried to remember if I had ever tossed my hair over my shoulder in that manner, but couldn't think of a time. I added this to my "to do" list.

Sorting out my thoughts and giving my emotions time to settle, I tapped a tune out on the tabletop. I was convinced if I found out whose land Will was digging on, I would get the evidence I needed to prove he found something that would cause someone to kill him. But I was open to other possibilities. What I hoped was to get the aardvark-slow sheriff to reopen the case, and then I could head back to my friends, my Grandma and my job. If I got the Lakewood's alone, maybe I'd discover Will was searching their land.

So shoot me if I hoped they were the killers. You'd think I'd want it to be Taco, what with her attitude and all. But she was young and naïve and merely standing up for Will after his death. I admired that, even appreciated it. Will deserved it.

In his letter Will mentioned that someone in the area knew a lot about pirates in Matlacha. I wondered if that was Jay Mann. After all, he did have those coins.

Taking my sketch pad from my canvas bag, I began to draw the faces of the Lakewood's. As I drew Esther's chin, I frowned. Someone was watching me. It was like the time I basted the turkey with vanilla instead of what I thought was teriyaki sauce. I'd known something was wrong, but I hadn't been able to figure out what until the turkey was served. I could feel the offending stare, but I couldn't locate the culprit.

I scratched the back of my head. Although it was 85 degrees, I shivered.

6

If I wake up in the middle of the night really, really bothered, I know a work isn't finished.

~ Robert Longo

Two hours later I bought staples at Winn-Dixie on Pine Island. As I left the store I made two phone calls. The first to Jay Mann: Dinner tonight at the Sandy Hook? Excellent. Seven? Perfect. The second call, to the Lakewood's. Esther answered and I told her that I knew no one in the area and that I felt a need to discuss Will's suicide woman to woman. Esther agreed to meet me at the only restaurant at the northern tip of Pine Island—Capt`n Con's.

I would phone the judge after I'd spoken to Esther. After all he had invited me to come.

Opening the trunk of my car, I slid the cold cuts, bread and yogurt into a hot/cold bag and started for Bokeelia long before I was to meet with Esther. After taking a curve, I pulled to the side of the road and walking, knocked on every house door, showing Will's picture, asking questions, getting few satisfactory answers. Only one person admitted seeing Will and that was in front of an art gallery. The man had had a conversation with Will about metal detectors. He said he thought he knew a lot about detectors, but Will knew much more.

"Did he tell you what he was doing here?"

"Sure did. He said he was digging for gold and when I laughed at him he grinned like a schoolboy. Excuse me for saying so, but he seemed a bit too happy. I told him there was a couple in the area who dressed up like pirates and told Bru Baker, a local pirate, stories and said he should get hooked up with them. He laughed and said he just might do that."

"When was this?"

"Well, that's the sad thing. It was before seven on the morning of the day he killed himself. I read about his suicide in *The Eagle* and Mary, at the post office, confirmed that it was the same guy. Made me sorry I made fun of him."

This sounded to me like Will had found buried treasure, confirming my theory. I straightened my shoulders and tugged down my tan cap for good luck. "Did he say where he was searching?"

"Nah, but I could tell he was at it. His shoes were coated with damp sand and the knees of his jeans were discolored and wet."

He offered to show the picture to his gallery visitors. Since I had brought several copies with me, I left it with him. I also gave him my cell phone number just in case he thought of some other detail or spoke to someone who did. Leaving, I congratulated myself on my logic. I was doing better than I'd expected gathering information. I retraced my steps, climbed back into my car and drove slowly to my destination.

I knew that Will was in the habit of keeping two sets of maps, but he never duplicated his logs. Since going to his apartment I'd been asking myself where he would hide the second map with no result. I parked in front of a dock that had a gate where the planks formed a T. Checking my watch and deciding I had time, I headed for the gate. A sign informed visitors that there was a fee to enter. What kind of person had to make money off someone just wanting to see a view or fish? I wasn't impressed. I retraced my steps and went toward the canopy entryway of the restaurant.

Esther sat in a dimly lit alcove drinking coffee. She wore a silk sundress that exposed her thin arms. Her brunette hair touched her shoulders. Sunglasses covered her eyes. "I see you were enjoying our dock?"

"Our dock?" I asked, pulling out a chair. Figures.

"After Harold retired and we moved here, he got bored and began buying commercial property. His plans were to raze this building and put up condos, but while the architects were squabbling, we got attached to it as is. We restored the dock. Coffee?"

Everything Esther said next about losing someone to suicide was the same as everyone said: It wasn't my fault. I couldn't have known. With time I'd get over the loss. I listened with lowered head and interlocked fingers. I didn't want this woman comforting me by holding my hand. Will may have been fooled by this woman's good looks and seemingly gracious ways. But I wasn't. This woman had "fake" written all over her.

Without waiting for me to speak, Esther switched the subject. She told me that she and Harold had had financial problems. Harold had invested too much in the housing market and everyone knew what had happened with that. By some miracle that Harold refused to tell her, he'd come out of it just fine. "I wasn't worried for a minute. My husband is a financial genius."

Of course he was. Didn't smart women always attract smart men?

I said I was glad things had turned around for them. So many people were still suffering financially. But I was strongly considering that perhaps, just perhaps the bailout money had come from proceeds of Will's treasure hunt.

Esther raised her chin. "A really, really good thing came out of it. I came up with the cleverest idea to help us out. Harold says the idea is a bit old-fashioned, but brilliant. Even though we no longer need the money, he thinks I should continue the project. He's so sweet."

She went on to tell me that she had recently begun to take on clients. The concept was simple: Take young, socially disadvantaged women and teach them how to survive in the cultured world of the upper, moneyed class, thus giving them a chance to find the right husband.

Whoa!

I was astounded, but I did my very, very best to hide it. I'd thought I'd heard everything. But this took the bouquet of roses for wacky ideas.

"Well," Esther said, "what do you think?" Her sigh defined melodrama.

No way was this the woman Will was interested in. Not for a split second.

No. Not.

But I decided when I got back to the room I'd practice her look and sigh in the mirror. Never knew when it would come in handy. And, of course, I realized it didn't matter what I thought, Esther was convinced she was a star in the business world. So I lied and said I totally and absolutely agreed with the judge: It was a clever idea. What I really thought was that it sounded like a scheme to take advantage of young women.

"What are your credentials for such a business?" I asked in my most sweet and innocent voice.

"Oh, I graduated from *Brown*, my dear, I'm an I 95er. Third generation."

I didn't know what an I 95er was, but I didn't want to admit that and show my ignorance of the East Coast upper class slang. Besides, I had something else on my mind, so I followed Esther's lead and did a fine job of swapping the subject. I might not have gone to an East Coast private school, but I knew how to take control. Life had taught me something.

"When we spoke yesterday, I had the feeling that you did speak to Will at Bert's. Am I wrong?"

Esther inspected her perfectly manicured fingernails. "This is just between you and me?"

"Absolutely." I leaned comfortably back against my chair and smiled directly into Esther's eyes giving her permission to be honest. Right.

"Well, I didn't want to say anything in front of Harold. He gets so very jealous. It's a husband's right, you understand, still…it's tiring. Wives certainly must learn to not tell their husbands everything. That's one of the lectures in my class."

Oh, no.

"Of course." What was amazing to me was that this dingbat seemed to be serious.

"Anyway, Will, on the day I saw him in Bert's, asked to talk to me in private. We went to the park. Taco had told him she was a new client of mine."

So, the Taco connection and the answer to why Will wouldn't be right for her at a later date—he wouldn't be rich enough. "And?"

"Will asked me to give her money back." Esther crossed her legs and straightened her skirt. She did not look at me, something I always take as a sign that the person is lying.

"Really?" I touched my throat. "What's the fee for your course, my dear?"

"Three thousand down. Twenty thousand after."

Whoa! What waitress would have this kind of money? Dollars? I almost blurted out, but instead said, "That sounds more than reasonable."

"Why, of course it is. I don't want my clients to think this is some kind of lower middle class operation. My dear, I went to *Brown*! If you don't know what that means, do look it up."

I now knew what it meant all right. This woman was a first-class, crazy-as-a-loon snob who had no idea how much money a waitress makes. Poor Taco.

"Anyway, the client pays the remainder after she gets married to a wealthy man, of course." Esther's smile was bright. Her chin rose even higher. My God! She saw herself on stage.

I swallowed a healthy portion of water and was reminded why people were driven to excessive drinking.

I just couldn't resist asking this question: "My goodness, how do women who are waitresses get the down payment?

Surely, they can't make that much in tips!"

Esther merely shrugged. "Borrow, I guess. That's not for me to be concerned about. If anyone wants to better themselves, they have to invest." Esther gazed at me with a look that told me who I was—a foolish peon. "There's no guarantee they'll find a man. I'm not a miracle worker, my dear. That's why the fee up front is so reasonable. Your man didn't see it that way. He said Taco had given me her life savings. He said I was taking advantage of her."   Esther, showing her outrage, pouted.

I did the best I could to keep my face blank. I was really, really having a hard time believing this woman was for real. "My, my, how thoughtless of him," I said. "What did you tell him?"

Esther's expression showed that she thought I was out of my mind. "I told him he was like every man I'd ever known. He didn't think women could think. He was understandably jealous of my idea. You know how men are. If the idea isn't theirs, it just isn't worth considering."

Clearly the woman was a deep thinker. Good grief! Not! "And he said?"

"I didn't give him a chance to reply. Men like that just don't get it. Why bother? Oh, I'm sorry, no disrespect meant." Esther swung her leg. "I'm sure your guy was nice and all. I just thought you'd like the full truth."

"I sure hope your husband didn't see you with Will. Men can be such beasts."

As can women.

"Why, how did you know that? He did!   And he was so mad. But, I think he is so sweet when he's jealous."

Motive: Jealous rage. It didn't take much to think that this woman could enrage someone. I'd already suppressed an urge to strangle the woman.

"But your husband said he had seen Will only that one time."

Esther frowned. "Yes, I know. That surprised me. I suspect he didn't want anyone to know how jealous he gets. He is a judge, after all."

"Oh, I see." Did this woman know she was handing me a motive in a silver bowl? Of course not. She had no idea I was investigating Will's death as a possible homicide. Or did she?

I warned myself to be less the questioner and more the grieving, vulnerable woman. Curving my shoulders, I adopted a pained air. And it worked. Woot!

Esther's demeanor softened. "Don't take it so hard, honey. Will wouldn't have killed himself if he thought you'd loved him and if you'd loved him you wouldn't have let him come down here by himself. Letting a man wander away is a huge, and I mean huge mistake."

How bad could it be to live in a six by six foot room? Once I'd visited a jail and found out they served pans of brownies, that books were delivered from the library and that the deputies did the inmates` laundry. How bad a life was that? But, I reminded myself, if I offed this woman I'd be in prison not jail. Probably no lovely brownies there.

I decided to accept that Esther was truly wacky and let it go at that. Again, making my expression blank, I smiled sweetly. "Another of your lectures?"

Esther looked demure. She nodded.

I gritted my teeth. "I'm sure your husband never acted violently when he was jealous? Like throw a vase or raise a hand to you? I mean, surely you warn your clients against this kind of male behavior?"

Esther gazed out the window. "Well, let's just say that I am very careful to not get him mad and I make sure my students understand the importance of being careful as well."

Whew! Be still my desire to karate chop.

Esther took off her sunglasses, showing a bruise below her right eye. A feeling of empathy washed over me. Instantly I wanted to take back all my sarcastic thoughts. It was one thing to think about using physical violence, but another thing altogether to actually hit someone.

"What happened to your eye?"

Esther touched her cheekbone. "I'd say I ran into

something. But that's such a silly cliché, don't you think?"

So he *was* a violent man.

"Oh, I'm so sorry. Surely, you've reported him?"

Esther puckered her lips, shook her head and replaced the glasses.

I understood that particular discussion was closed. "What happened that day when your husband saw Will and you together?"

"Oh, the fool came storming at Will and pushed him against a palm tree."

"Really? Poor Will. He was so very non-violent."

"Oh, I could see that. Well, I screamed, like any sensible woman would and he told Will he'd better never see us together again. Then he grabbed my arm and dragged me to the car. Such unnecessary melodrama. For heaven's sake, I was only talking to him!"

"Oh, my! I hope no one saw this exchange?"

"Thank goodness, no. We were in an isolated area. That was part of the problem. Harold didn't think we should be there. I was very embarrassed. Afterward, Harold apologized. He always does." Without a pause, Esther announced she was going to Sanibel shopping and asked me if I wanted to join her.

I, acting terribly, terribly disappointed, declined, using an appointment as my excuse. "By the way, I was wondering…the night of Will's death…was there a big crowd out front when the ambulance arrived? I mean, I hate to think of him being seen like that and all. I know he'd be covered in a sheet, but really…the idea is so dreadful."

It was almost as if Esther were waiting for this question, she answered so quickly. "I totally understand, my dear. I can't imagine anyone seeing Harold like that. But, Harold and I went to a show at the Barbara Mann Auditorium, so I can't say. We stopped for dinner afterward at our favorite Thai restaurant in Fort Myers. We didn't get home until after twelve." She glanced at her watch, and then raised her hand for the bill.

I leaned back. "Thai food? Oh, one of my favorites." Not!

As I was sure she would, Esther gave me the name of the

restaurant. I asked if she would have more time for me in the future. Without hesitation, Esther agreed, said she'd enjoyed herself and after paying the bill, left.

To calm myself I remained for a half hour sketching a portrait of Will. Often I used my drawing to get rid of pent up emotion and it usually did the trick. This time it was asking a lot of my drawing.

Before leaving I showed my sketch to all the waitresses and the woman at the cash register with no result. I left my cell phone number and the sketch. Outside I telephoned the Lakewood land line and the judge answered. He was happy to see me. I only hoped he wasn't a husband on the make. All vanity aside, I'm not that bad looking. Men tend to watch me as I walk across a room. It must be the long legs and auburn hair that catches their attention. I do tend not to wear low cut tops that would show off my 32 Bs. My Grandma Murphy did teach me something. She was old-school Irish, through and through.

Parked, but remaining in my car, I phoned the sheriff's office and asked to speak to him again. "Yes, Ms. Murphy What do you want *this* time?"

For this auspicious occasion, I purposefully chose my woe-is-me voice; that one usually worked with men of the sheriff's age and disposition. "I was chatting with Will's sister and she was asking if I knew what time Will was killed. She said she was having her horoscope read and her brother's time of death was important. I, of course, couldn't provide that. Would you be so kind as to help a woman in distress? She would be eternally grateful, I'm sure." I made my sigh loud and long. "Oh, and Millie said to tell you hello." I imagined the sheriff was blushing as he thought of the woman who had evidently captured his penile interest in one brief, sad encounter. I almost added that Millie, Will's sister (I'm sure using the first name gave him an orgasm) suggested he should stop in to see her sometime when she was in Sanibel, but I'd save that line for another time. A man could only take so much pleasure.

"Oh, that poor, poor woman. Just a minute and I'll get the

file."

My head buzzed with the effort it took to hold back my anger.

He gave me the information within minutes. "Yes, well, you tell that poor woman the time of death was estimated to be between 10 and 10:30 p.m. Now you'll make sure she knows I gave you this information, right?"

"Oh, definitely, Sheriff, and I am sure she'll be very appreciative. Thanks so much."

Some men are just so predictable. Now to the judge.

The Lakewood's lived in a luxury condo, or condos, as the judge was quick to point out. He owned the building and had turned two of the units into one, giving them five thousand feet of living space. The décor had a wealthy, Italian flair. The disappearing pool backdrop was Charlotte Harbor. I couldn't help but notice that the large terracotta pots held imitation silk plants. How utterly classy.

The furniture was dark-brown wicker. The two white upholstered sofas were oversized, as in mega HUGE. I was sure the Oriental rug cost more than I'd make in a lifetime.

The judge was dressed in a flowered shirt and khaki shorts. He wore leather sandals and his tan was deep and even. I wouldn't have been surprised if there was a tanning bed in the place. I didn't ask for a tour and was glad, but surprised when he didn't offer one.

His welcome was warm and didn't send any wrong signals. Ready for any quick move, however, I took the seat offered, but sat on the edge. After all, I was in a house with a man who I suspected killed Will and this guy weighed close to two-fifty. I weighed all of one-twenty.

The judge went to a marble bar and took down two glasses. "Gin and tonic?"

It was 11 a.m. Now I knew that he and Esther had been married for quite some time. Surely, she had successfully driven him to a life of excessive drinking. No surprise. I, on the other hand, had serious business to attend to, so I asked for tonic and lime only. I made a habit of not drinking before noon. A beer with lunch was acceptable, but nothing else until after five.

While he made his drink, I asked a question designed to keep the visit on ground I controlled. "I was wondering if you heard anything about Will to suggest he was depressed. As you may imagine, his suicide came as a complete shock." I reached for the glass of tonic.

"Let me think. As I told you, I saw him only that one time." He sipped his drink, eyeing me over his glass.

I had the uncomfortable feeling he was assessing me like a piece of property. I wondered what price he would put on me. I shifted my body away from him, but he continued to stare and my discomfort deepened. I set down my glass in preparation to leave. It would have been wiser to meet this guy in a public place since I planned to accuse him of lying about how many times he'd seen Will. Hawk would be livid. This guy could be a killer, after all. We were alone. Even Gar was absent. Oh, dear. I clamped my mouth shut.

Mr. God-Complex cleared his throat and stopped inspecting me. "There might be one thing."

"Yes?" I began tapping out a tune on the arm of the chair. Catching myself, I intertwined my fingers.

He dragged his attention away from a picture of a naked woman on the wall. "It's rumor, mind you. And rumor is nothing but gossip. It has nothing to do with fact. But, I did hear that your man and that older woman bartender at Bert's had quite a falling out."

"Do you mean, Lil?"

"I believe that's her name." He twirled the ice in his glass.

"So, Lil and Will had an argument?" I asked, distracted by the whirling ice.

Interesting how everyone pointed a finger away from themselves.

"Rumor, mind you," the judge said, touching the back of his head.

I reached in my bag, pulled out a tissue and dabbed at my eyes. "Argued about what?"

"I'm sorry. I really don't know."

I sniffled. Nice touch, huh? "Who told you this?"

He eyed me. "Unfortunately, it was one of my dearest friends and poker buddies who overheard the argument."

"I'd love to talk to him. Every time I speak to someone who knew Will, I feel closure inching nearer." I blew my nose. Daintily.

"Oh, I'm so sorry, my dear. For you and for me. He had a heart attack last week. His death is such a great loss."

Liar. Liar. Speedo on fire.

I dabbed my eyes again and put the back of my hand on my forehead.

"Are you okay? Perhaps this is all too hard on you. You poor dear."

"No, no. I'll be fine. I just need closure so badly. Could you tell me where you were the night Will was killed?"

The judge visibly bristled. "Why, you sound like a cop."

Whoops! I chided myself for asking too blunt of a question. Squeezing together my eyebrows, I made my eyes look pained and amazed. I'd perfected that look in an acting class I'd taken in college. "Oh, dear, no. Me? How funny. I watch too many cop shows and, oh dear, how rude of me. I guess I picked up their way of asking questions. How funny you should think that." I made a sound, somewhere between a giggle and a groan or a moan.

He still wasn't convinced. "And you asked that particular question because?"

This called for super drama. I dropped my head into my hands and faked a sob. "Oh, I don't know. This is all so hard to accept." My shoulders slumped. I trusted I came across as pathetic. If I didn't I was going back to that acting instructor and complain about his teaching.

The judge set the glass on the bar. His voice was softer. "That's okay, my dear. I know you're hoping beyond hope that Will Rolins didn't kill himself. No one wants to think someone they cared for would commit suicide. It's so ugly and makes one feel vulnerable. To answer your question, although why it matters, I can't imagine, Esther and I had gone to some God-awful musical in Fort Myers at the Barbara Mann Auditorium. Boring. Dreadful stuff."

I raised my head, making sure my expression remained pitiful.

But I was thinking it was unfortunate that their alibis matched. That didn't mean they hadn't rehearsed what they were going to say when the question was asked. Asking if they'd gone to eat afterward would be out of the question, so I swallowed that urge and thanked him. I stood to leave. The judge walked me to the door. As he reached for the handle, I said in an off-handed kind of Colombo way: "Your wife is very beautiful."

Long pause. Reddened face. Clenched and un-clenched hairy fingers.

Hit a nerve. No doubt about that.

He did a chest puff then said in a controlled tone meant to put me in my place, "You really do seem to be fishing. If by some wide stretch of the imagination, you're imagining Will was killed and I did it because he and Esther had an affair, I'd put that directly out of your mind."

Did this man really think my Will would stoop so low? Shame on him.

"Oh, I would never suggest that. Will would never..."

The judge looked at me sharply. "Good day, Ms. Murphy."

I couldn't blame him for being upset. Hadn't I just acted like a detective and more or less suggested he might be a killer? I'd be irritated too if that had happened to me, but I wouldn't be too understanding to the jerk. After all, he was a wife beater and a greedy sucker.

When I arrived at my car, I climbed inside and locked the doors, pondering what I had learned. Had Will fought with Lil too? Doubtful. But if they hadn't fought, why would the judge want me to think that they had? And why hadn't he told me about seeing his wife with Will and being upset by what he saw? Had Esther lied? Possibly. How long would it take to get from the Barbara Mann Auditorium to Will's duplex?

I had lots to do.

In a surprise weather move it rained all the way back to Matlacha. As I stepped onto the dock of the motel, wind swirled and whirled across the water. The sea slapped against the pilings and broke up and over the dock. I ran, unlocked my door and shut it, then went to the window. Boats rocked. A chair tipped over.

Moving to the nightstand, I lit the lamp. It was 6 p.m. and already dark. Seeing Gar was a comfort, however, I couldn't shake the feeling that the weather was foreshadowing danger as I hurried back to close the window. A red and yellow table umbrella somersaulted across the dock, cracking against the railing then sailing over the confused, raging water. An orange life jacket smacked the side of the building then disappeared.

My monkey ringtone began to laugh and I jumped, chuckling at my nervousness.

"Hello."

No answer.

"Hello."

The line went dead.

Catching my lower lip between my teeth, I sat on the edge of the bed near Gar.

If someone was trying to scare me they were doing a damn good job of it. If I heard an owl hoot I was out of there. Owl calls were used in scary movies for a reason.

7

I shut my eyes in order to see.
~ Eugene Henri-Paul Gauguin

At 7 p.m. still rattled by the phone call, I stepped into the restaurant where Jay was waiting for me. Big and strong. Capable of taking on a speeding bullet in his rolled up sleeves and khaki pants. I was surprised with how relieved I felt when I saw him.

As we were taken to a window table, he spoke in a warm and welcoming voice. "I'm so glad you telephoned. I was rude when you came to my house. Please accept my apologies."

"That's quite all right. I was the one who was rude. I did come unannounced. The shock of Will's death has me forgetting my manners."

"Sudden deaths are very tough to deal with. If I can help at all, I'm more than happy to try."

The waiter came, took our drink orders, brought the menus and left. Fixing my eyes on Jay I wondered if he had a family. "Thanks. I really do appreciate your concern. You seem like the family type. Am I wrong?"

Jay's gaze left my face. His look darkened. "I was. My wife left me for our doctor and took our girls with her."

Crap. Like how could I put my foot in my mouth any deeper? "Oh, dear. How dreadful. Do you see the kids often?"

"Not at all. She poisoned them against me."

"But surely the courts…"

He didn't allow me to finish my sentence. "She hauled them off to England. The last time I went to see them they wouldn't even come out of the house."

"Oh!" I was speechless. What terrible things people do to each other.

"I should have fought for custody, but I didn't want to put them through that. My mistake."

"I'm so sorry."

He said nothing and I turned my head toward the window. Someone had carved unused pilings into totem poles and painted them. The moon cast a rippling line. The effect was one of a lit path leading to the horizon. I thought of Robert Frost and his poem about paths not taken. How many people choose suicide when they are hit with the tragedies and disappointments of life? Why does one choose death and another choose life? I glanced back at Jay. He, too, was gazing into the night. What does one say to such a travesty? I couldn't imagine having kids and not being able to see them.

Breaking the awkward silence, the waiter arrived to take our orders. When he left I decided the best thing to do was to direct the conversation to Will. "I hope you don't mind if we talk about Will?"

"Please do."

"Thanks. Stop me if I'm too blunt. It's a bad habit of mine."

He nodded.

I continued. "I was remembering that you said Will didn't seem depressed when you last saw him. What about when you first met him?"

"Hmm. Seems to me that first night in Bert's he was very talkative. By the time I had to leave I knew he wasn't sleeping, his appetite had all but disappeared, and that sex didn't interest him much. All classic signs of depression, true?"

Create a shield, girl. You're right. They're wrong. Yet, this did sound like he'd stopped taking his medication. Please, don't let this be suicide. "Will *was* on anti-depressants," I finally said.

Jay, at first, was silent. When he spoke, he appeared to be weighing his words. "Maybe he…stopped…taking them?"

I buried my head, fighting for emotional control.

"I'm sorry, but it's a possibility?"

I nodded but said nothing. Our eyes locked as the waiter delivered our food.

Jay seemed to be trying to recall something. "Ah, I remember now. Will called us kindred spirits."

I smiled a thin smile. "That sounds so like Will."

Jay and I discussed the idea of having connection with other humans we'd never met before. Jay, too, had had this feeling more than once. Believing in the concept of Law of Attraction was also something we had in common. As we talked we leaned closer together across the table. We seemed to notice it at the same time. We straightened and picked up our glasses.

"How long have you been in Matlacha?"

"Ten years now. At first I rented and thought I'd head for Key West. But after a couple of weeks, I realized I'd found what I was looking for."

"And what was that?"

"A spot that gave me inspiration for my work."

"I know exactly what you mean. I feel it too. The creative energy."

"I've never been able to put my finger on what exactly it is here that appeals to my muse. But that's okay. Whatever it is, it works and that's what's important."

"So you own your house?"

"Yeah, I bought it before prices skyrocketed. I also own a lot in Bokeelia. I thought I would build on it, but, well, that never happened either."

I wished he hadn't said that. Although he was on my suspect list, I now didn't want to suspect him. I liked him, and more importantly, I felt sorry for him. What with the loss of his kids and all and his wife's treatment. I felt like a low life, but I had to pursue. "Did Will ever ask you if he could dig on your property?"

Will frowned. "Dig? Why would he?"

"You didn't know he was a treasure hunter?" That was really hard to believe. Will was the type who spent hours alone, but when he got around people, he talked fast, he talked often, and he kept few secrets.

"Really? That's news to me. No, he never approached me about that."

I raised my wine glass, missed my mouth and dribbled merlot down the silk shirt I'd found at a garage sale for a quarter. "Hey!"

Picking up my napkin I dipped into my water glass and rubbed. This was my best blouse—the only one I had that could be considered dressy. "I assumed you'd know," I said, continuing my clean up job. "Matlacha is a small place. Both Lil and Rose at Bert's were aware of his digging." As were the Lakewood's. Why not Jay?

A large wet circle highlighted my right breast. I spread my napkin on my lap.

Jay suppressed a grin, almost. "As I told you, Will and I only saw each other briefly and he certainly didn't mention this. And I'm not exactly friendly with most people in this town, I'm afraid. I'm out of the gossip loop. A treasure hunter, huh? Interesting."

"It was his passion. This was his third hunt."

"I see. This is certainly the right place to come. Lots of pirate treasure around here."

"I was wondering if you remembered what time you saw Taco and Will talking the morning of his death."

"Hmm, what time? Well, usually I have a late breakfast so the place isn't so crowded. Oh, yes, I remember. I was to have coffee at 10:30 that day with a friend from Fort Myers. I arrived just before she did. Taco and Will were leaving as she came in the door." His gaze flicked to my damp breast where I was positive the outline of my nipple was visible, then to my eyes. "You sound like a detective. Correct?"

I put my hand over my breast. "Me? Oh, no. But I did work for a P.I. for a few months and I guess I developed the habit of gathering details. Habits are hard to break." I reached for my water glass, caught the side of my wine goblet and it tipped again. "Whoops!"

In a flash, Jay reached out and grabbed it. I crinkled my nose and thanked him.

"Yes, well…"

The breast thing was really bothering me, so I excused myself and headed for the restroom. I stuffed some folded toilet paper into my bra to provide camouflage for the nipple, then talked to myself about being too pushy with my approach. Too many people suspected my motives.

I inspected myself. Ewww. Not good. I added stuffing to the left breast. One really shouldn't be off-balance. A woman entered the room as I was withdrawing my hand from under my shirt. I didn't look at her. When I returned to our table, for the sake of keeping my cover, I spoke of a safer topic, pirating.

Jay told me that many people talked about the pirates that used to live in the area, but said certainly he was no expert. He suggested I speak with the woman who worked behind the counter at The Olde Fish House Marina. He didn't know her name. We ended the evening by discussing art (one of my favorite subjects) and how difficult it was to keep the muse.

Jay offered a ride to the motel, but I refused, saying I preferred to walk. But, in truth, I had one more thing I wanted to do under the cover of dark—something that I thought of while reading Will's letter.

Although it was nighttime, it was still around eighty degrees. I went toward the community park and the tiny broken seashell and pebble beach where Will said he had been swimming nightly. Perhaps Will had left a clue that would lead me to the truth tied to a buoy that he said he swam out to. A sailboat was moored off shore. A lone crab buoy bobbed up and down. That had to be the one. The sweet scent of jasmine from a nearby climbing bush wafted through the air. A bevy of seagulls swept the water and flickered away. Seeing no one on board the boat, no one walking the path behind me, I took off my clothes, laid them on a bench and in my bathing suit waded into the water.

Several feet out I raised my arms and dove. When I surfaced, I was holding a yucky damaged crab trap. Feeling all around it, I found no note, no map or log in a plastic bag. Disappointed, I let it drop.

I counted each stroke, swimming for shore in the line created by the moon. Four feet from land, I stood. Water lapped at my chin. A pelican landed on a dead tree branch. Walking backward, arms spread wide for balance, toes sucking the gooey bottom, I stepped onto the shore. The pelican stayed put.

With a loud thud I plopped onto the beach, and like a soaked otter, flipped my head from side-to-side. With my eye on the pelican, I lay back on the sand, placed my arms to my side and began scissoring my legs while raising and lowering my arms.

The pelican extended its wings and flew away.

I positioned my hands under my head. A great blue heron moved regally across the sand. I closed my eyes and thought about Will and our relationship.

Wrapping my arms around Will's shoulders I had often told him that I loved him. The night before he'd left, he said, "I couldn't live without you, woman. You know that, right? My life began when we met."

Oh, Will.

Gazing into the sky I located the constellation, Delphinus, west of Pegasus. Delphinus, the Dolphin Constellation had been the God of the Sea, Poseidon's messenger. He, a perfect sidekick, had succeeded in persuading Amphitrite to marry him and move to his underwater realm.

"Hey, Delphi, can you help me too?" I whispered into the night sky.

Footsteps crushed on the gravel and seashell path. Alert,

aware that all my questions could have raised suspicions and that I was a woman alone in an isolated place, I sat up and grabbed for my clothes.

The footsteps faded. I quickly dressed.

My eyes narrowed and my jaw tightened. I was only a romantic to a point. Flighty, I was not. A bit zany, yes. I *had* after all once called the hood of a car a lid. But incapable of being reasonable? Nah. I may not have a mythological god at my disposal, but I had my mind, persistence and determination as my armor, and I had Gar. Standing, I walked fast back to the motel room, and immediately made a timeline of what I knew about Will's last day:

Before 7 a.m. seen in Bokeelia, excited.

Around 10:30 a.m. seen with Taco coming out of the coffee shop, animated conversation.

Not wanting to add the last thing I knew, but hated to admit, I hesitated a long time before writing: Since Will was manic-depressive, this could mean that he was off his meds.

Fighting my sadness, I stretched out on the bed and picked up another letter.

"Okay, I can do this. *'Dear Weiner, I've been discouraged these last couple of weeks.'* Oh, great. He *was* down." Why hadn't I noticed all these mood swings when I first read the letters? Simple, because I didn't want to recognize them. I wanted alone time.

I held up the letter. The words seemed to sizzle. *It's hard to keep the faith when day after day you find nothing. If I were someone else, I'm sure I would have quit this madness a long time ago, but this is my current passion—this crazy hunting for buried treasure. That's why I've always been surprised that you gave up your painting. I mean, I know you have to make a living. I know I am lucky—what with the trust fund and all. But, still, with your talent, can't you find more time to use it? I'm sorry. I know I'm harping.* Oh, Gar, all he wanted was the best for me. Why couldn't I have just accepted the lifestyle he offered?"

Not enough faith in myself as a painter. Competition too

stiff. Too many better than me. Desire to not be taken care of by a man.

Gar, of course, remained silent. But I knew what he was thinking...Stubborn woman.

"Don't worry about it, Will would called me stubborn, too"

I read some more, then said to Gar, "Will says Matlacha is full of people we should meet. Jay Mann, Rose and Lil, but there's another guy here that he says we'd like, Luke Abbot. He owns the Islander Gallery and some of the things he shows remind him of that painting over our sofa. The last one I painted. When was that? I...God, I can't remember. Gar, these letters just keep pushing for me to come down here. Oh, Gar..."

Why, oh why, did I wait so long?

I set down the letter, picked up the judge's note card and added the words: Jealous rage when seeing his wife with Will. Lied about seeing Will with Esther. Said Will and Lil argued. Another lie? On Esther's card, I scribbled: Is that wacky business of hers a front for something else? Did Will find this out, confront her and was killed? On Jay's card, I wrote: Why didn't Will tell him about his treasure hunting? Suggested I go to the Fish House to get info about pirates.

I went to the open window. The night was now calm. The man was visible in the moon. I listened for human noises on the dock, but none came. Waves lapped against the pilings. A bird swooped low. Whiffs of sea stench made my nose crinkle. I closed the window, dressed for bed, pulled back the comforter and slid under the sheets. I turned off the lamp. Moonlight lit up the room. Putting my hands behind my head, I watched a spider weave a web in one corner. The gossamer threads were so fragile, ethereal, so easily destroyed. The monkeys began to laugh. I reached toward the nightstand and picked up my smartphone.

"Yes?"

No answer.

"Yes? Who's there?"

The phone went dead...again.

I bit my lip and slid the phone under my pillow. Someone didn't like me asking questions. I hoped that was the case. It would mean Will *was* murdered. Which he was, I assured myself.

I scooped up Gar and nuzzled all seven pounds of him under the covers. I'd hate to hurt Gar, but he'd do quite some damage if I hurled him toward someone's head. I had, I was proud to say, been a pitcher for my high school softball team. And if whoever was threatened got close enough, there was always my karate to fall back on. I wouldn't sleep. Not for some time. I switched on the light and picked up Will's letters.

Tomorrow—the art gallery and Luke Abbott.

8

As an artist, it is central to be unsatisfied. This isn't greed,
though it is appetite.
~Lawrence Calcagno

My fifth morning on the island dawned gray and gloomy,
causing me to want to stay in bed. Making myself get my sorry
butt up, I dressed grumpy as a gray-haired curmudgeon in heat.
I'd had two-three hours steady sleep max. Outside, everything
looked different—less welcoming, more ominous, coated with
a gray mist. As I pumped my arms I passed several people
fishing on the bridge, but I didn't smile. Instead, I focused
straight ahead, determined to get my three miles in. Sweat
streamed down my forehead. My cap stuck to my hair. My
heart pounded, keeping rhythm with my step. A horn honked.
A truck skidded. I felt itchy, almost needy. What did I want?
Will's killer found…yes. But that wasn't it. And it wasn't just
because I needed more sleep. Or that I was being targeted by
some sick prankster.

The exercise didn't improve my mood as I had hoped.
Head down, I returned to the room, ignoring Gar. Longingly I
gazed at the unmade bed. But climbing back in this early
seemed pointless. I pulled off my sweaty clothes and dropped

them on the floor.

After showering and dressing I headed out again, leaving Gar behind. I walked across the bridge and strolled to the Islander Gallery. The building was a historic one-story fisherman's cottage now painted in bright aqua with blue trim. Near the open front door, a cement mosaic table and two benches screamed whimsical.

I wasn't in the mood for whimsical. But, oh well. One can't always have what one wants.

The floor I put my pink flip flops on was made from more multi-colored, chipped pieces of tile. Part of the mosaic was in the shape of fish, others in the shape of tropical birds. I stood holding my therapeutic drawing pencils and a sketch pad like an aimless zombie until a friendly woman appeared and startled me by her greeting. I blinked and half-smiled. The room was lined floor to ceiling with photographs, acrylics, watercolors and pen and ink drawings. Brightly painted furniture held finely crafted wooden boxes, hand-thrown pottery, and sculptures in copper, brass and steel. A case was filled with jewelry made from copper wire. Handmade bamboo woven dolls of various sizes rested on the edge of most surfaces. Gourds were painted in scenes so tiny that I couldn't take my eyes off them. Furniture was transformed by Florida landscapes. Stylized fish, pelicans and a wall-sized caricature of Van Gogh decorated another room. Feeling my mood shift from bad to not so bad, I asked the young woman behind the counter if the owner was in and was told to sit out in the back and she would have him find me.

Spreading open dangling strings of glass beads, I stepped out onto a patio. Meandering tiled walks, tropical plants, and an abandoned wooden dingy filled with coconuts didn't exactly make my fingers itch to pick up my drawing pencil, but seeing the canal farther back was more promising. I moved in that direction.

I sat under the shade of a fuchsia-colored bougainvillea-draped arbor and tilted my tan cap back. A yellow and green parrot in a cage watched my every move. If he starts talking to me, I decided, I'm out of here. I really wasn't in the mood to talk to a bird, no more than I was in the mood to talk to Gar, or even to Luke Abbot. Keeping focused on the brackish water, I began to draw the mangrove and the turquoise boat in the narrow channel. Gradually not so bad turned into pretty darn good. I'd found my zone. When I was in my zone, my soul soared.

With time the sun came out. I continued to draw.

A shadow fell across my page. I reluctantly put down my pencil.

"Hi, there." The man's face was chiseled out of granite. His eyes were blue-green. His silk shirt showed off his broad shoulders. His white shorts made his muscular legs gleam. He was the kind of guy who made a woman catch her breath and I, even in my state of mourning, was no exception.

I cleared my throat and closed the sketch pad.

He held out his hand. "Hi, I'm Luke Abbot, the owner of this charming establishment."

I nodded. "And I'm Jessie Murphy, the girlfriend of Will Rolins."

"I'm so glad to meet you. I wanted to tell you how sorry I am for your loss." His other palm covered my hand and felt as rich and silky as his empathy. "Lil and Rose said you sketched," he added. He released my hand. "I'm glad you came in. Is this the sketch book I've heard about?" He pointed to it.

"This is the tablet I draw in…yes."

He sat on the cement bench in front of a glass tree made from a wire base, large railroad spikes and blue wine bottles.

"This is a charming, whimsical gallery, Mr. Abbot."

"Luke, please." He glanced at my notebook. "Mind if I see your sketches?"

I slid them toward him. He opened the cover and inspected each page. Expressions of interest and pleasure appeared on his face, making my mood rise even higher.

"So, will you turn these into paintings?" His smile could melt a memory stick and had most certainly thawed my last shreds of funk.

I pulled my thoughts away from his perfect lips, knowing how much it would please me to recreate them on canvas. "Perhaps."

"Your medium?"

"Oil."

He turned another page. "Intriguing angle of the head. I'm very fond of pelicans myself." He closed the book and twisted his body toward me. "I'm always looking for new talent." His eyes were earnest and magnetic.

Thrilled, in fact, almost overjoyed with his words, I used the most nonchalant, intelligent word I could muster. "Hmm."

"Would you mind if I took a look at any paintings you might create? We have a Coastal Weekend Art Night coming up and I could use more art on my walls. I take 40% of all sales."

I almost jumped up and did a jig right then and there. Was he kidding? Would I show a man who owned an art gallery my work? You can bet your darn buttudy I would.

"Well…sure…." I said in my best, casual voice.

Gar, wait until you hear. You won't believe it! Oh God, I think I'm going to be sick. Okay. Okay. Focus on why you came here. Remember your purpose for being on the islands. I straightened my shoulders and spoke in a quiet tone.

"I hope I'm not becoming a pain, but do you mind if I talk about Will?"

"Not at at all. This has to be a difficult time for you. The world is a lesser place without him." I almost loved him for those words.

"I keep reminding myself that it's only his body that's gone, that his soul will live forever. But it's hard. I've begun rereading his letters and had the impression he was friends with Jay Mann, the sculptor. I was surprised when I learned that Jay wasn't one of his friends."

"Yes, well, Will didn't like Jay that much."

"Really? Now that's a surprise. In one of his letters he said he did." It was at that point that I realized I hadn't remembered mention of Jay again in any correspondence after the first one. But I needed to double check this to make sure my mind wasn't doing tricks on me.

"I think you're right about that. They did hit it off at first. I saw them a couple of times at Bert's. They seemed real chummy. I don't know what happened to change Will's opinion. But I know Jay was angry and showed up in a sad state at a party that Will had."

"How angry?" And why?

"He showed up drunk and disrupted the party, trying to pick a fight with Will."

"Odd. Jay doesn't seem like that kind of guy. And Will was no fighter."

"I know. We were all surprised," Luke said. "No one seemed to know the cause of the problem."

A man wearing a green and yellow fern-patterned shirt strolled to the table. Luke placed his hand on the man's arm and introduced him. Luke explained they had an appointment and asked me to phone him in the near future if I had further questions. I assured him that I would. The men excused themselves. "Oh, and please think seriously about getting a painting ready so I can take a look." He tossed me another one of his million-dollar smiles and the men walked away.

With a concentrated effort, reflecting on his request, I redirected my dazed-with-wonder attention to a cormorant that landed on the edge of the coconut-filled boat. It spread its wings and began drying itself. Did it know how amazed I was with the interest in my work? So, I'm superstitious. Shoot me. I stood and forced my thoughts to return to what I had just learned from Luke about Will.

So Will and Jay argued, and Jay didn't tell me this. Interesting. Did the argument have anything to do with Taco? Why wouldn't Will like Jay? Because he mistreated Taco? Jay didn't seem the type. Nor did Taco seem like someone who couldn't take care of herself.

When I left the gallery I was smiling. The sky was bluer. The palm fronds greener. My flip flops slapped the wooden planks of the motel's dock. After taking time to inhale some salt air, I turned and unlocked my door.

I stretched out on the bed and pulled my smartphone out of my pocket to phone Hawk. "Hey, there. How are you?" A fly was trapped in the spider web overhead.

Hawk said he was fine then asked, "So, are you learning anything that makes your decision to stay worthwhile?"

"Tell you the truth, I think Will found treasure and was killed for it."

"Oh, Jessie, do you know how hard that is to believe?"

"Yeah, well…" I avoided looking at the fly. I liked Hawk, but he often said I was more right brain than left brain, more the zany artist than reasonable private eye. This irritated me thoroughly, especially since I'd never done anything with my art. It was probably part of the reason I'd quit his agency and become an apartment manager, to hone my practical skills and sharpen my reason-based gray matter.

"Listen, I've got a copy of the report you asked for, he said. "I can either send it snail mail or flag it to you by fax."

I certainly had no idea where I could receive a fax and didn't want to wait for the delivery. "Can you read it to me?"

"Are you sure you want to hear this?"

"It's okay, Hawk. I know the reports are explicit."

"Make sure you're lying down. I haven't had a chance to read this yet, but I know there's nothing soothing about these things."

I reached over and drew my finger down Gar's wing. "I am, with Gar beside me."

"Good. Here goes: Thirty-two-year-old male is victim of apparent suicide. The decedent appears to be victim of self-inflicted gunshot wound. The body of Rolins was lying on his back on the floor of his living room near a desk. There was what appeared to be a bullet hole in the side of his head and a pool of congealed blood had formed under the body in the area of his head and shoulder." Hawk paused. "Want to hear more?"

I didn't. You can sure bet I didn't. "Go ahead," I said in a soft voice. He continued. "Pinholes were noted in the wall over the desk where it appeared something had been affixed. Photos were taken and everything was gone over for fingerprints. Water was removed from the traps of the bathroom and kitchen sinks. Gun was bagged, samples of blood stains were taken, and other physical evidence was gathered and labeled. Sounds like the forensic team did a fine job," he added.

And I, without realizing I was doing it, let out a prolonged, dolphin-like noise.

"I think I should come down there," Hawk said. "You need some support. Something's fishy. Pinholes. A revolver we both know Will would never touch."

I thought about my suspicion that someone had been near my door, and the feelings that someone was watching me, the phone calls. I should tell him about those, but I didn't. I was fine. Stubborn? Yes. But fine. I could handle things on the island by myself.

"Now, Hawk…"

"Don't give me that stubborn act. I know you. You wouldn't tell me you're in danger if I asked. Let me rephrase that, I *am* coming down there. But I can't catch a flight until I finish this case. Can you stay safe until then?"

"You really don't have to…"

Hawk didn't let me finish. "I'm coming. Just not sure when. Got that?"

I knew that no-nonsense tone. No use arguing. "Yeah, sure. In the meantime could you see what you could find out about these people?" I gave him the names of the Lakewood's, Jay Mann, Taco, Rose and Lil and asked if there was any way to find out if Lil was recently awarded a divorce settlement.

"Anything's possible. I'll get back with you soon. But listen, any signs of danger and you'll call the police, right?"

"Absolutely," I said, picturing the wing nut-eared sheriff and grimacing as I patted Gar on the head.

"Jessie, I mean it!"

"I said I would, didn't I?"

After saying our goodbyes I put my phone on the table

beside Gar and turned him so that he faced me, glaring at him. His expression told me what he thought of me not telling Hawk that I was already feeling threatened down here. I raised my chin and stuck out my tongue at him. "Oh, shut up, hairball!" I swirled him around.

I shot a look at the small stack of letters. Picking up the last one, and ignoring the salutation, I began to read out loud:

"I met this guy on the drawbridge, but turns out he lives right next door. He fishes with shrimp bigger than my thumb. But the most interesting thing is that he knows all about pirate lore. Talking to him is like getting an infusion of adrenalin. If I start to falter in my resolve, he's the guy I go look for. But he told me something last night that really ticked me off. I was tempted to call the authorities, but Gator (quite a name, huh?) said not to bother. The guy was already under the Fed's eye. You know how I think I'm such a good judge of character? Well, my dear, I missed this one—100%."

I chewed on my thumbnail. Was Will referring to Jay or possibly the judge or someone else? Did one of them have a deep, dark secret? Will had written nothing else about Gator's revelation. Will, I knew, wasn't that good a judge of character, even though he liked to think he was.

I returned to his words:

"The longer I'm down here, the more I'm convinced that lots of people come to Florida because they've had trouble up north. My dad used to say that when I was a kid over in Miami. Everyone seems to have a scheme. Nothing is what it seems. Gator says the con man is the only man down here."

Hawk often said the same thing about Boston.

"He seems disappointed, doesn't he, Gar?" Poor, Will. He always wanted people to be more than they are. "Listen. There're two places I'll take you to when you come, a spiritual center and Demere Key. Get this: In the mid-1800s pottery shards and tool fragments were discovered that showed prehistoric man had settled on Demere Key. The key also held unusual remains of a Calusa temple mound. The wooded key had once been surrounded by a massive, twelve-foot seawall constructed mainly of whelk shells. Apparently there were six shell mounds around 1895, and one of the larger mounds had a flat elongated top or truncated pyramid. Altar-like platforms were discovered. It's thought that Demere Key was used as a worship place or a holy spot where sacrificial victims were offered to the gods of the Calusas. Burial places were also found. Sometime in the `50s a lodge was built at the end of the key on a flat-topped shell mound. I'm trying to meet the residents to see if we can get invited for a visit. It's privately owned and off limits to strangers or treasure hunters like me. That's it for tonight, Weiner. I'm dog tired, Butternut."

I put down the pages and added the two locations he mentioned to my list of places to look for clues. But first, Gator, the man with pirate info.

My eyelids lowered then closed. I yawned.

An hour and a half later, closing and locking my door, again leaving Gar to mind the store, I walked down the narrow dock and headed toward the drawbridge, only steps away. As always, men and women lined the railing, fishing. Amazed, like Will had been, at the size of the shrimp being used as bait, I stopped to speak to a woman with a cigarette dangling from her mouth.

"Look! Dolphin!" I exclaimed as a pair surfaced, disappeared, resurfaced. I addressed the woman, speaking in a matter-of-fact voice. "You haven't seen Gator around, have you?"

Behind us a truck skidded to a stop, horn blaring. I hesitated, waiting for the sound of metal crashing into metal. None came.

"Not yet," the woman said, baiting her hook.

Another woman in a straw hat passed us and nodded.

"Hey there, love!"

The fisherwoman chuckled. "That's him," she mumbled. "Can't miss that voice."

Someone was calling a woman 'love'. Oh my God! How utterly British. I just love the British. They're so proper.

A barefoot man in jeans, a muscle shirt, a scraggly beard

and a tattered straw hat walked toward us. Will would have called his sudden appearance synchronicity. I called it downright disappointing.

"Les said a northern pretty gal in a tan cap was looking for me. My guess is it's you."

Pretty gal! Oh, my. I just might have to think about moving down here permanently.

I soon realized that Gator was the other occupant of the duplex where Will lived. He had also been at Bert's the night I'd arrived. Lil had made some comment to him about making a pest of himself. I put out my hand and introduced myself. Gator's handshake was firm. I unfortunately crinkled my nose when he came close and couldn't help but step away. Gator had a cloying odor, an overpowering co-mingling of cigarette smoke and dead fish.

Gator noted my reaction and grinned. "Don't worry, love. You ain't the first gal don't like my body smell. I ain't bothered. Come on over here so we can talk." He led me across the bridge to two empty chairs in front of a hole-in-the-wall convenience store next to a bait shop. "This is my office," he said. "Make yourself comfortable."

At the risk of offending him, I slid my chair a couple feet away while Gator pulled out a pack of cigarettes, offered me one, and when I refused, lit it for himself. "Just wanted to tell you I'm sorry about your fella. He was a real nice guy."

"Yeah, he was." Again I was temporarily silenced by kind words describing Will; as always I worked at controlling my emotions. When I felt I could speak in an even voice, I said, "He mentioned that you two talked a lot."

Gator scratched his face. "Oh, I wouldn't say that he did that much talkin`, but he sure did listen real good. He was usually pretty tired from diggin` by the time I saw him."

"He said your pirate stories motivated him."

"He sure did like hearin` about the pirates."

"Uh, I was wondering, did you get any notion that he might have found treasure?"

"Now, that's a mighty interesting question. `Cause I did

see him earlier that night and he was walking real fast. Had a bounce in his step. I got the feelin` something was up. That's why his suicide came as such a shock. I would've sworn he'd found somethin`, but guess I was wrong."

"Did you tell this to the sheriff?"

"Sure did, but he said I must have been mistaken. He had no doubt it was a suicide."

Okay, so I was going to tell a lie. I was glad my old nun teacher wasn't around. "There's another thing, Will mentioned you gave him information that changed his mind about someone, but he didn't mention what or who it was. Would you mind telling me about that?"

Gator leaned his head back and blew two smoke rings before answering. "Told him we got us a seeder in our midst."

"A seeder?"

"Yep. That's someone who seeds sunken ships with old gold coins and the like in order to entice investors to invest in a dive. Quite a lucrative, illegal racket—`til you're caught."

"And this seeder is someone Will knew?"

"Oh, yeah, the seeder is pretty well known." Gator blew another smoke ring then raised and lowered the cigarette like a fan.

"Why hasn't this seeder been arrested?"

"Feds are biding their time."

I knew a tall tale when I heard it. I watched an osprey fly to a nest and land. "Ah, not to discredit your story, but this sounds like a wild imagination at work."

Gator shrugged. "You believe what you want to believe."

I played along. "So, who's the seeder?"

"Sorry, love. That's for me to know and you to find out. Feds warned me to keep my trap shut or they'd throw me to the sharks."

Oh my! This was rich. "Ah, come on! Feds don't…"

"Like I said, love, believe what you want."

Gator refused to give any further information.   I left convinced the story was fiction. The important thing, however, was that apparently Will *had* believed this man. Will was gullible. Maybe he figured out who Gator was referring to. Will would never have been friendly with anyone involved in illegal activity.

Recalling again the old coins in Jay Mann's studio, I wondered if he could be the so-called seeder—thus the answer to a friendship nipped before full bloom. But I dismissed the idea immediately. The guy hadn't seen his kids in ages. Poor man.

9

Experience, even for a painter, is not exclusively visual.
~ Walter Meigs

As I crossed the bridge under construction a light wind caressed my cheeks. The sun cut through the disappearing mist. An osprey with a fish dangling from its beak flew overhead. The sea smelled like the dead. My tongue tasted like I'd been taking Fenadol for a year, salty and violated. Someone once said, "The problem with Florida is the sun always shines." Well it sure hadn't most of the morning.

I'd been here five full days and it was hard for me to speculate how long it would take to get concrete evidence that could be given to the sheriff so he'd re-open the case. I didn't know how long I'd expected to be gone from Cambridge, but I knew I couldn't stay more than two weeks without putting my job in jeopardy. I needed the money to pay my bills. I really, really needed to find something that proved Will was murdered. Reluctantly, I put those thoughts aside. Sometimes I found if I allowed things to jell without dwelling on them, an answer materialized. I'd try that.

I leaned over the bridge railing, not far from Island Avenue. Matlacha was not like classy Sanibel, an hour boat ride away or was it glitzy, neon-lit Fort Myers Beach, or the bedroom community atmosphere of the nearby Cape Coral, nor the academic, urban atmosphere of Cambridge just under fifteen hundred miles north. It had an artsy-fartsy, funky down-home flavor. And I liked it.

I thought of what Luke Abbot had said about my work. How Will was always encouraging me to paint. How I was expected to be painting while he was down here hunting for treasure, but hadn't. And just like that, as if a light bulb went off in my left always-pulsing gray matter, the sudden urge to paint was overpowering. Not giving the light bulb a chance to dim, I high-tailed it for the motel.

Tripping over the doormat, I asked the Indian desk clerk for directions to the nearest art store. Taking Gar with me, I drove to Cape Coral. I bought a staple gun, canvas, paints, mineral spirits, a palette, brushes, charcoal and another sketch pad. The supplies felt like little nuggets of gold.

Later, positioning stretcher bars, I tapped in wooden wedges and leaned the frame against the dresser. Spreading out the roll of canvas on the bed, I measured and cut, making sure the canvas was at least three inches bigger than the wooden form. I started stapling in the center. "Rose. Lil. Taco. Esther. The judge. Jay. Which one?" I said out loud.

Intuition told me Luke and Gator weren't involved. Sympathy made me want to keep Jay off the list, but I settled for reason not feelings. An act that made me think I was being at least objective, if nothing else. Which for me was something.

I shot in four staples. Stretching the canvas taut, I pressed again. Stretched. Pulled. Worked out from each side, center to edge. When I had each section like I wanted it, I folded over the ends, pressed down and finished the job. Leaning the canvas against the dresser, I inspected my handiwork and decided it was just fine. Like riding a bicycle, once you know how to prepare a canvas, you know.

I set up my easel on the back dock. I never knew what would happen when I began to paint. That was the beauty of it.

The not knowing as I followed my inner urge and let my hand have free reign with the paints. It was such a cool feeling, being in my very own speed zone…with no limits or stop signs. It had been too long. My blood boiled. It was a natural high. I saw and heard nothing out of the tiny space created between my easel, my palette and my brushes. Hours passed.

A loud whoosh near the dock caught my attention.

I set my brush and palette on my stool, hunkered down and held out my hand. The manatee swam closer. Smiling I stretched forward and the water sent sparks through my fingers and up my arm. The manatee had disappeared. I glanced around. A white pelican sat on a piling, preening. "Did you see her?" The pelican raised and lowered his wings. But no manatee. The pelican quivered his reply and seemed to grin at me. My shoulder muscles relaxed. I stood, and leaving my work unattended, walked down the dock. Turning the corner, I strolled all around the motel, unhurried, relaxed, like a long-legged great blue heron on a beach.

When I returned the pelican was still there. I thought he would be. I went back to work.

I remained on the dock so long cars no longer whizzed by and all other guests had gone in and closed their doors. Crescent moon. Stars bright, dazzling, intense. But the manatee did not return and the white pelican never left.

Carrying my nuggets of gold into the room, I set them on the table near the door, then hauled in the easel and canvas. The pelican skimmed the gleaming, radiant water, heading in the direction of the moon. "See you tomorrow," I whispered.

"Yoohoo! Jessie! You comin` to Bert's tonight?"

Rose's cheeks were painted with blush. She was festively dressed in a red pant suit with sequins and high heels.

"Why, look at you. You look super!"

"Thanks. It *is* New Year's Eve." Rose eyed my shorts and T-shirt. "You've got something better than that to wear, I hope!"

New Year's Eve? Really. I hadn't realized.

I chuckled. Who Miss Second-Hand-Woman-Me? "Sure. I

brought a couple of dresses. I'll change. Come on in."

Rose stepped inside and went right to the canvas on the easel. "Hey, I told Lil and Luke you'd be talented. That's what I said."

I mean, I just loved these kinds of words. They were like strawberry jam on toast. Or deep, dark chocolates made with real cream and butter. So easy to swallow. But the painting wasn't anywhere near done. Even I had no idea where it was going from here. I thanked her and went toward the closet. "It's just a pelican." I pulled out a yellow-flowered dress and held it up. "

"How's this?"

"Perfect." Rose pointed to my unfinished painting. "Now, this thing would sell. Wait till I tell Luke." She lowered her voice. "I heard you met him."

She had heard already? What an impressive communication system on these islands. Grandma Murphy used to say the same about her dinky town.

Rose crossed her arms over her chest and inspected the painting with interest. "Luke was charmed with you and your sketches. He said he couldn't wait to see a painting." She looked from the canvas to my face. "Why! Bless my soul. The pelican has Will's eyes!"

I blinked rapidly.

"Oh, hon, I'm so sorry. You go ahead and cry if you need to." Rose stepped toward me and encircled my shoulders, pulling me close.

But determined little me shook my head and stepped aside. "I'm okay, Rose."

I was afraid if I accepted comfort now I'd fall apart and give away my purpose for being in Matlacha. I couldn't do that. It would complicate my investigation. Steadying my rapidly beating heart, I went into the bathroom. Not taking the time for a shower, I wiped my face and armpits with a washcloth, rolled some deodorant on and changed into the dress. "You must have known Will pretty well," I said through the closed door.

"I suppose I knew him better than anyone else. He used to stop by my place at night before I went to work. Of course, he was only in Matlacha a short time, so no one knew him well."

I stepped into the living area.

"How beautiful you are. Ah, to be that young again."

I blushed. No wonder I liked the place. Not only was someone interested in looking at my artwork, they kept complimenting my physical appearance. Will had never said anything about how I looked—ever. And I never knew until that moment that getting compliments could make you feel real good about yourself. Real good. I mean, not that I had low self-esteem or anything. I knew I wasn't hard on the eyes. It was just that having someone like Rose and even Gator...well...it just made me feel good. That's all. I slipped into flip flops and opened the outer door. "What a night. Look at that cucumber-shaped moon. Will would have loved this."

Rose squeezed my arm. I squeezed back. As we walked down the dock, I continued to talk about Will. "Besides hunting for treasure, I wonder how Will spent his time down here."

"I used to see him standing on the bridge gab boxing with Gator. Once I saw him go out with Jay on his boat. I know he used to read a lot. And, by the way, I never did see him sashaying around Taco. I know gossip has it that he was. Oh, they were friends, but it sure didn't seem like they were lovers, and they sure wouldn't have any reason to hide the fact if they were. Who would care?" She groaned. "Sorry! You would, of course."

I pressed my lips together. "Why do *you* think Will killed himself?" We circled a parked car.

Rose turned her head so I couldn't see her face. An action that I noted. "I don't know, hon. I don't think anyone will know the answer to that," she said in a distant way.

We went around an idling truck.

"I take it you're off work tonight?" I asked. Like, duh! Dumb question.

Rose grinned. "Yeah. And Bill is dropping by. Lucky me.

Come on, I'll buy you a beer."

We stepped inside. Several people were wearing party hats. Holiday lights sparkled. Voices hummed. The wooden pelican near one open doorway had on a green paper hat with cascading multi-colored ribbons. A band was in full swing. The odor of frying fish, fries, and decades of beer scent and sweat rained down on everyone's head. Rose and I exchanged a look of amusement and weaved through the standing-room-only crowd toward the bar. I had to raise my voice so Rose could hear me. "I heard a rumor that Will and Jay Mann had an out."

"Oh, yeah," Rose, speaking over the noise, went on to relate the same story I had already heard from Luke. She added, "When Jay fell in the gravel and skinned his hands, he threatened to get even. He's not the type who likes to be snubbed. I mean, I don't like the guy."

"Sorry to hear that."

A male waiter I had never seen before put two glasses of beer in front of us. "On the house." His eyes lingered on me before he moved away.

"Thanks," Rose called. "He likes you," she said, eyeballing the room. Turning to look at me, her eyes hardened. "About your question, we're waitresses. Jay Mann looks at us like we're dirt. He's full of himself. Lil believes he thinks being a Christian and Georgia Cracker like I am means I'm ignorant. Getting ignored by women like us doesn't bother Jay Mann. Not like being ignored by Will would of. Jay thinks he's some hotshot artist. I guess not being invited to a party Will had hit a nerve."

"It seems weird to me that Will wouldn't invite him to a party. Will was a live-and-let-live kind of guy."

"Who knows? Mann probably deals in drugs and Will found out. How else does he live so high off the hog? He hasn't worked a day since being here."

"Maybe he sells his art."

"Yeah, right. Like that would pay the rent."

Maybe, I thought, but didn't say and wished I hadn't

thought, he makes a habit of stealing. "So, when was this party?"

"The Friday night before Will…Well, before he died." Rose's expression brightened. "There's Bill. Be right back."

Lil came out from the kitchen, wiping her forehead with the back of her hand. "Whew! I'm getting too creaky for these long hours!"

"Hey, you're only as old as you think."

Lil snickered. "Out of the mouth of a pup." She asked me to turn around. "Look at you, all dolled up and all."

"You don't look so bad yourself. Nice duds." Lil had on a black shimmering, low-cut blouse and skin tight jeans. Her eyes continued to sparkle.

"Quite a crowd," I said.

Taco, in a revealing white top and shorts shorter than short, slipped out the door balancing a tray full of beer bottles over her head.

"Lil, what do you think was going on between Taco and Will?"

"They liked each other, I know that—did a lot of chattin`."

Rose and Bill came and stood close to me. Bill was talking about his grandkids and how he had played Santa for them. I avoided looking at him. How could she possibly like this ugly, gruff guy? Amazing.

"God has a special place for you in heaven," Rose said before they put their heads together and their words were lost to others.

Lil swiped the counter with the bar rag and asked me, "You ever have kids?" At the question, Rose's head lifted.

"Nope," I said.

"Having a baby is sacred. God loves `em from the time they're conceived," Rose added.

Lil rolled her eyes. Arm in arm, head touching head, Rose and Bill walked away.

"I wouldn't talk abortion with her if I were you. It's a touchy subject, as you might imagine. I had an abortion, but I wouldn't tell Rose. She'd probably have me fried in hot grease."

Will and I were pro-choice. Will was quite vocal about his stand. Me? Not so much.

"That extreme?" I asked innocently, watching Rose and Bill laughing.

"Extreme doesn't touch it," Lil said. "That woman would as soon shoot you if you even thought of ending a fetus's life. Like I said, don't raise the subject with her. It could put her heart out of rhythm. Rose has a faulty valve." Lil was called away. I was left contemplating pro-life violence and other leads.

As I said, the place was crowded. I don't do well in crowded. Rose was busy with Bill. Lil was busy working. I just wanted to return to my room and kiss Gar at midnight. So I left, contemplating my next move. Hopefully, the Thai restaurant that the Lakewoods supposedly went to after the Barbara Mann performance was open on New Year's Day.

Tomorrow I'd investigate the Lakewoods` alibis and work at finishing my painting. The following day when the library was open, I would check on pro-life violent activity on the East Coast. Didn't Rose say she had traveled up and down the coast? Rootless. I thought that was the word she used. Next I would check on possible seeding activity in the area. Could Will have decided Jay was a seeder? Oh, yeah. I'd already let Hawk see what he could find out about Lil's alleged settlement. Good. He should be here soon.

In my room, turning Gar toward my easel, I took out my paints and brushes. I squeezed out a generous dollop of blue, burnt umber, black and white and continued to work. "Lots of possible motives: jealousy, greed, hate crime." I said to Gar. "But no proof."

I mixed some gray, then stood back and inspected my work. "What do you think, Gar?"

But he wasn't listening. Just like a man.

10

I cannot expect my own art to provide all the answers—only to hope it keeps asking the right questions.

~ *Grace Hartigan*

It was a new year and I was painting. I couldn't believe it. I dropped my cleaned paintbrush into the blue Ball jar and stood back from the easel. Overall, I was pleased with how the piece was evolving. The canvas no longer contained a realistic portrayal of a pelican, a realistic anything actually. I kept reminding myself that I had nothing to prove with my art—that what others thought didn't matter. But still, if Luke accepted this and it was displayed, there would be critics lurking in every corner. Ewww. Double ewww. Of course, I could always not finish this, which was my strongest urge.

There was only one thing I hated more than art critics, dumpsters. And that was my Grandma Murphy's doing, because when I was five she told me if I ever, ever touched a dumpster she wouldn't buy my warts. And I knew if she didn't do that, I'd have warts all over my hands until I was old enough to use a walker. I knew that because she assured me it was true. And if there was one thing my grandma didn't do that was lie. Cause if you lied…well…I won't go into that.

But, believe me, I genuflected and crossed myself several times when I was forced to lie.

Picking up my tan cap, which I hoped was still lucky, I put it on and left the motel. The Thai restaurant was in a small strip mall near Orange Grove off Hancock Bridge Parkway and easy to find, especially since I used my trusty GPS.

It was 12:30 when I arrived and several of the tables were occupied, which was a good sign the food was at least edible. I'm not much for exotic, foreign food. I'm more of a meat and potato type of woman. I headed for a table near the back and sat opposite the door holding tight to the notion that by doing so, it was better to see who might want to shoot me—a habit I'd picked up from Hawk. `Course there were times I wondered why I'd want to stare a shooter in the eye. I mean, wouldn't it be better not to see who was going to put out your lights? But Hawk was my boss and I believed everything he taught me. Just like I believed most things I read. Unless it was downright dumb of course. Which many things were.

An olive-skinned man with a friendly smile and demeanor came to the table before I had a chance to look around. He asked for my drink order and gave me a menu. He didn't seem too disappointed or disapproving that I only ordered water. For food, I asked for his recommendation. His face softened in pleasure as he named several dishes. I ordered a cup of soup, salad and main dish before extracting two things out of my pocket. First, I showed him Will's photo. He said the guy looked familiar, but that was all. When I handed him the sketch I'd done of the Lakewoods, his smile broadened.

"Ah, the Lakewoods. Very nice."

I kept my expression blank. Were we talking about the same couple?

I asked if there was any way he remembered the night of December 18th when Andrea Bocelli had performed at Barbara Mann. I figured it was a long shot, but hey? What the heck.

"Oh, yes. Mrs. Lakewood and I had the most delightful conversation about Bocelli. He's my favorite crossover singer. I'd been to his performance the previous night. Mrs. Lakewood seems to love him as much as I do." He glanced over his shoulder. More tables were now occupied. He bowed slightly and excused himself.

It wasn't until I was having a cup of decaf after the meal that he was able to stop for more than a moment at my table. I took the opportunity of asking him if he remembered how long the Lakewood's stayed for dinner.

"Oh, they were one of the last to leave," he assured me.

Closing time, I had seen on the front door, was 11 p.m. Since Will had died sometime between 10:00 and 10:30 p.m., the Lakewoods` alibis were tight. Of course either of them could have hired it done, but that seemed too big of a stretch. No matter how much I disliked this couple, I had to admit they probably weren't the killers.

Since it was New Year's Day I decided to go to the beach on the way home. I'd brought my suit, an umbrella and lots of suntan lotion. I switched on the radio and as usual my upper body began to sway to the music as I drove onto Hancock Bridge.

Gar kept his peace.

The Caloosahatchee River was choppy. Few boats were out. A car behind beeped. I frowned at the rearview mirror. The driver was waving. I slowed down. The car sped up. I broke into a wide smile. It was Luke Abbot. I waved back, pulled my cell from my pocket and held it up, pantomiming that I would call. He shook his head and then passed me. I followed until after leaving the bridge he pulled into a parking lot. I turned in and parked, rolling down my window.

"I knew that was you. I left my phone home or I would have called. Where're you going?"

I grinned up at him. "To the beach. I feel like some sun."

"Super. Me too. Which one?"

"Bowman's on Sanibel."

His face lit up. He leaned closer. His aftershave had a sweet, pungent smell. "Mind if I join you?"

I told him I'd welcome the company and that I had more than enough food for two. He returned to his car and pulled to the back of the parking lot. Lifting his trunk, he hauled out a canvas bag, brought it to my car and opening the rear door, tossed it in beside Gar whom I had just moved. "You always seatbelt him?"

"Of course."

Five seconds later we were off.

I knew I was still grieving, that my grief was seeping into my drawings and painting. Creating had always been a great way for me to vent my feelings. But I didn't plan to turn Luke into my therapist. "One thing…"

"Yes?"

"No talk of Will or creating or your gallery."

He assured me that was more than fine by him. Glancing at his handsome face, I couldn't believe my luck. Lots of people like to be alone. I need plenty of solitude myself. But on a day when you feel like the beach, having human company rocks. We remained for several lovely minutes in companionable silence. Every time my mind switched to a Will memory, I forced it away. It wasn't easy.

"Hey, you're not laughing," Luke said.

"What?"

"You weren't listening to me. And here I was being so charming."

"I'm sorry. You're right. I was self-absorbed, a bad trait of mine. What were you saying?"

Luke retold a story that had me laughing all the way to the turn-off to the Sanibel Bridge. He insisted on paying the toll. We sailed across the bridge with a pelican following on either side of the car. Low. Slow. Lovely dinosaur throw-back beach guides. A steady breeze blew through my hair. Not a cloud in the sky. A yacht sounded its horn as it passed. A slice of heaven.

Luke, apparently enjoying his role as a story teller, kept me entertained all the way to the beach parking lot. As I unloaded my gear, he went to the *Park and Pay*. Opening the back door, I pinned my gaze on Gar. Normally, I would take him to the beach, but with Luke here, well, I guessed that Gar would be just fine remaining out of the sun. I snatched up the Frisbee from the floor and patted Gar on the head. Once Luke had his bag, we strolled down the crunchy pathway leading to the bathhouse and the Gulf.

I felt good. Something I hadn't felt since coming.

At the lagoon, we stopped and leaned against the railing, gazing out over the mangrove-lined brackish water. "Don't you love this?" I eyed a white cattle egret.

"Yeah, what's not to love?"

We smiled at each other and moved on.

At first, after spreading out towels, we undressed down to our bathing suits, applied generous sun block—I applied some to his back and he did the same to me. We sat, facing the sea. The hair on Luke's chest was blonde and curly. His back was broad. His fingers were long. I wore a white bikini; one I had spent more money on than the rest of my year's wardrobe—and my tan cap. Our long legs stretched beyond our beach towels. I pulled up mine, buried my toes in the sand and wrapped my arms around my knees.

Three seagulls stood nearby watching us. A dozen or so sandpipers scurried toward the water. Whitecaps broke, creating surreal, quick to vanish images in the dark folds of the sea. Directly in front of us, two dolphins were fishing. One jumped, tossed a fish into the air, caught it and disappeared. A family of four under an umbrella to our right, clapped. Peals of laughter rolled down the shore. I buried my fingers into the fine sand and leaning back, raised my face to the sun.

"Wanna walk?" Luke stood and extended his hand.

I allowed him to help me to my feet. We were the same height. We gazed out to sea. A flock of pelicans glazed the water's surface. I pulled my cap lower.

With one of my feet in the water as we walked, I kept my eyes on the tide.

"Ah!" Luke bent quickly and scooped as the water rushed backward. He straightened and palm up, opened his fingers. "A lightning whelk."

"Alive?"

"Glad to say it isn't. Here, a gift."

The shell was about one and a half inches long. One end resembled a crown. The other came to a fragile rolled point. Delicate ribbed edges added a washboard texture to the center. "It's beautiful."

Our eyes caught. My cheeks reddened. I ducked my head and ran.

"Hey, wait for me!" Protecting the shell in my hand, we jogged down the shore passing sunbathers, two young boys fashioning a sand castle and a lone man in a beach chair reading under an umbrella. I lengthened my stride. Luke did the same.

"Race you to that point," he said and he was gone.

I yelled and dashed after him.

I was gasping by the time I took my last step toward Luke, who was also bent over taking in deep breaths.

We returned to the towels slowly, hesitantly, sluggish as snails, neither talking, just enjoying the moment. Only by concentrating on the shell grasped between my fingers, could I keep my mind from drifting back to Will.

I laid the shell near my bag and took out two bottles of water, offering one to Luke. "It's so good to have a day like this. Leaving everything behind."

"Amen."

"You religious?"

"Oh, yeah," he said. "Not a fanatic or anything. Just believe in God." He glanced around. "In a world like this, why wouldn't you believe in a higher being?"

I had to admit, I got it. Nature was like some big-ass teacher that kept trying to tell you something. Hey, airhead, get your head out of the sand. I'm here all around you. Take off the blinders. But I didn't say this to Luke. Instead, I let his comment pass, reached into my bag and pulled out an over-sized sandwich. "Hungry?"

He smiled. "You bet."

After eating, we reapplied sun block, played Frisbee and then stretched out for an hour. After a swim, where we were joined by three women in their late fifties, we packed and soon were driving across the bridge again.

"Jesus! Look at that?"

"I'm driving. I can't see. What is it?"

"A boat just hit a sandbar. You should have seen it come down. That boat will never be the same. Some boaters just don't watch their charts."

11

An artist lives everywhere.
~ Greek Proverb

The next day I was standing outside the library admiring the stunning image the sun's rays were making on a dark green native Coontie when the door was opened. It took me no time at all to get a temporary number so I could use the computers. I logged in and within seconds was on the net. What I found on the first site gave me goose bumps.

Since the early eighties abortion-related violence had occurred all up and down the East Coast. Everything from nail bombings, to shootings to anthrax mailings.

How could people kill others or threaten lives when they professed to being pro-life? It was really, really hard to swallow. But if you believed in good you had to believe in evil. And I believed in both.

I clicked on another link and learned the National Right to Life Convention had met in Jacksonville in July. That was only a five and a half hour drive. Just how involved was Rose in this cause?

Next I read about the Army of God. As a Christian terrorist anti-abortionist organization that sanctioned the use of force to combat abortion, they'd been active since 1982. Members had kidnapped and finally released an abortion doctor and his wife.

An East Coast division of the AOG claimed responsibility when three men planted bombs at seven abortion clinics in Maryland, Virginia and Washington D.C. in 1985.

And there was more and more and more heart-sickening information.

I closed down the web.

As I walked out the front door, I pulled out my cell phone and called Bert's asking for Rose. Would Rose join me for a walk? She would. Rose suggested we meet at 11:30 at the west tip of Fort Myers Beach. She said she needed some beach walking time and would enjoy having my company. We could drive together, Rose added, but she had a meeting to attend in Fort Myers at one o'clock. I knew the spot. Will and I had gone there on two different quiet Sunday mornings.

I was surprised when I found a parking place. It was tourist season, after all. Rose was sitting on a bench near the water. She saw me and I waved. We both wore shorts, flip flops, sleeveless Ts and hats. It was 84 degrees and the sun was high in the sky.

After greeting, we strolled in companionable silence before Rose said, "I'm glad you called, girl."

I smiled at her and breathed in the salt air, knowing that on another day, under different circumstances, this could be a perfect moment. The water was smooth as a marble granite top. Two boats idled past. Birds soared overhead. The scent of rotten organic matter mixed with the fainter smell of gardenia blossoms made me feel so alive, so very human. Times like this confirmed my belief in a higher power. I bent to pick up a sand dollar. It was the size of my palm, light to the touch and had not been damaged. I slipped it into my right breast pocket and glanced at Rose. Suddenly repulsed with what I thought her capable of, my mood darkened.

An egret oblivious to our approach strolled along the water's edge. A mother with a baby strapped to her front passed us. Rose cooed, giving me the ideal opening.

"I got a call last night from a young friend of mine," I lied.

"Yeah?"

"She's planning to get an abortion."

Rose froze. "How dreadful!"

"I know. I've done everything I could to stop her, but she won't listen."

"Does she live in Boston?"

"No. Charleston. It's a terrible situation. She was raped and can't bring herself to have the child."

"That's still murder."

I turned away pretending to be interested in a hibiscus blossom. "I know," I said. "Life begins at conception."

Rose wrapped her arm around mine. She appeared to be deep in thought as we followed the pebbled path. A trawler pulling a dingy motored past. "I'm confused. Will was totally pro-choice, yet you say you are against abortion."

Thanks to that acting class I did a convincing job of hardening my expression and my voice. "Dead against," I said. "You can imagine how frustrating it was for me to know that Will thought such nonsense. It just made me sick to see that pro-choice sticker he put on his car. We argued about the issue constantly."

I patted myself on the back.

Rose nodded. "So did we. That man just wouldn't change his mind. He was infuriating. Why he even…" She let her sentence drift away, released her grip on my arm and quickened her step.

I blanched and lengthening my stride caught up with her. "He even *what*?"

"Oh, nothing, girl. It's not important. I won't talk bad about the dead. Hon, if you get me the name of the clinic the girl plans to go to, I might be able to help her make the right decision."

"Really? How?"

Rose slid a stray strand of hair away from my right eye. "Just leave it to Rose, hon. She can perform magic."

Rose wouldn't say anything else about the topic and I

promised to get back to her with the information she requested. She had to run. The meeting, remember?

Following a hunch, I decided to tail Rose.

Practicing caution I remained three or more car lengths behind Rose's Cavalier. Luckily, the lights were with me; I didn't lose her as we traveled along McGregor Boulevard. Rose turned left into the Town and River sub-division, bore right at a Y in the road and parked on the grass behind a long line of cars. Either the meeting was packed or other neighbors were entertaining as well. I pulled into a driveway of what seemed to be a vacant house—badly taken care of yard, lifeless plant in planter near door, window shades drawn. I parked the car behind a silver-leafed Bismarck palm and watched as Rose hopped out and headed toward the house next door from where I had parked. The circular drive was also lined with cars.

I jotted down the address of the house, plus several license plate numbers. What next? As far as I knew, this could be a Bible discussion group or a volunteer meeting. It could also be a secret rendezvous of the Army of God. That thought made me cringe. How could I find out what was going on without putting myself in an awkward situation? Dang. I wish I'd brought Gar for moral support.

I inched open the car door, slid out, pulled my tennis shoes and socks off the back seat and switched my blue flip flops for walking shoes. Closing the door quietly I pushed my hair into my cap and lowered the bill to better cover my face. That, with my large sunglasses should do the trick. I raised my arms and began to power walk, but not toward the house Rose went into, away from it. Establish that you're a walker in the neighborhood. Look like you belong, I told myself. Hope that Rose doesn't look out the window and recognize you. At a rapid, arm-pumping pace I moved even faster than usual. At the end of the street, I crossed over and reversed direction. Stopping at my car, I opened the trunk, took out a water bottle and drank until it was empty while keeping my eyes on the house. So far so good.

Rose must have been one of the last to arrive. No new cars

came. The street was quiet. I finished the water and dropped the bottle into the trunk. Nonchalantly (well, that was the way I hoped I was projecting at least) I slipped around the empty house and confirmed my assumption. The house had been vacant for some time. The pool water was brackish and weeds needed to be pulled around the screen of the lanai. I could hear voices from the house next door.

I opened the abandoned lanai screen door and stepped onto the pebbled patio. Crossing the stone I hid behind a half wall. The house next door was less than five feet away. I heard conversations almost as well as if I were part of them. Putting my back against the stucco wall, I slid to a sitting position and listened. A man was speaking: "I say it's time to make another move. Too many babies are losing their lives."

A loud, many-voiced murmur followed. I made out several harshly spoken words: abortion doctors, embryo-killing research, gay devils.

Again, I felt heartsick. I clamped my hand over my chest.

To my alarm a small dog started to yip and yip and yip.

I slid up the wall. Swiftly, remaining out of sight (I hoped), I re-crossed the patio, tiptoed out of the screened-in pool area and made it to my car without an incident. Swallowing my anxiety I reversed and headed back for McGregor Boulevard, the toll bridge, Cape Coral and then Matlacha.

Would Rose have killed or had Will killed for his beliefs alone? That didn't make sense. But there was no doubt that Rose was a member of this violent group. A police car passed. I touched the brakes. My leg went up and down. I tapped on the steering wheel. I took out my cell phone to call Hawk, but changing my mind, pulled into a Publix parking lot. I found their wall phone and dialed 911 and left an anonymous message that a suspicious, possible terrorist meeting was being held at the address I gave. I ended by giving them the license plate numbers.

When I returned to my car I gnawed on my lower lip until it hurt. I would really, really, really be glad when Hawk arrived. Things were getting a bit too scary.

I shifted into gear and burnt rubber.

12

Art doesn't transform. It just plain forms.
~ Roy Lichtenstein

That night at Bert's nothing was said about Rose or a raid on a home in Fort Myers, nor did the news include such a report. I was puzzled, but kept my thoughts to myself as I watched Taco sashay toward my table.

"Lil asked me to talk to you," Taco said.

Thank you, Lil. "Excellent. Can you sit?"

Reluctantly, Taco lowered herself into a chair. "I got work to do. Get to it."

"O…kay." No reason to be subtle. I leaned on my arms covering my drawing tablet. "Esther Lakewood tells me that you're a client of hers."

"Yeah. So?" Taco's eyes remained averted.

"She told me all about her business concept and, well, I think it's wonderful—what she's doing for young women and all."

Taco licked her lips and acted as if whatever was going on at the other end of the outside eating area was much more interesting. "You're kiddin`, right?"

Be cautious, girl. Step lightly.

"Why, not at all," I said, using my most sincere tone. "Why do you say that?"

"Guess I assume you'd think like Will. He thought it was all bullshit and he told Mrs. L to give back my money. I wasn't impressed, him butting in and all."

I leaned back. "I'm sure Will thought he was doing you a favor."

"I suppose." Taco studied her fake, red fingernails.

"I think everyone deserves a chance to attain their dream," I said, actually believing that surely there were better ways of doing it.

"Me, too. Too bad your man didn't think that. I was afraid Mrs. L would drop me as a client. Luckily, she didn't. That it?" Taco pushed up from her chair.

"One more question. Is this what you were talking to Will about the morning of his death?"

Taco's eyes narrowed. Slowly, she sat again. "Not that it's any business of yours, but since it's the second time you've asked, well—we were talking about abortion clinics."

I didn't hide my amazement. "Abortion clinics?"

"Yep. A friend of mine needed to hook up with one and Will overheard me asking if anyone knew where one was. We started to talk and Will assured me that in many cases an abortion was the best decision. He even told me how to find a clinic. I was sure glad he had common sense on that subject."

Wondering if Rose knew about this I watched Lil deliver two fish baskets to the nearest table. How easy it would have been for Lil to hear our conversation. As if she read my thoughts, our eyes locked and Lil's face reddened, before she turned her back and weaved around a couple going in the direction of the cash register.

I slid my cap toward the back of my head. "Anyone within earshot when you were talking to Will?"

Taco shrugged.

"I don't suppose you remember who was in the café?"

"God, my nails are a mess."

"Taco!"

"What?"

I repeated my question.

"As a matter of fact, I do. Rose and a couple of tourists. Jay Mann had just left. It was a quiet day."

Rose—the anti-abortionist.

"And did you see Will again?"

Taco sighed. "Afraid not. I had to work all day and then had supper with my parents."

"So Will didn't tell you that he found buried treasure?"

Taco raised her eyebrows. "Why, no. Did he?"

I had hoped for a different reply. Disappointed, I shook my head. "I don't know. I was hoping that he had."

"Sorry. As far as I know, Will's dream was a pipe dream— like most dreams, I might add." Nodding curtly, Taco resumed her edgy demeanor and returned to the bar.

A lone, abandoned sailboat was moored and listing to the right. Had Will sat at this table looking at the same boat? Had he seen the mast rising high out of the center, saw its ignored splendor? Had he questioned why no one tried to retrieve it? When we first met, Will would have attempted to restore that boat, spending hours bringing it to a thing of beauty. But then he became fascinated, obsessed with the idea of buried treasure. Will—the man who often was disappointed. Who went from gleeful to gloomy in the course of a day.

To my surprise Rose walked into the bar. Seeing me she waved and motioned. "Hey, come out here!" She slipped out the side door.

Rose was standing at the railing. The words on her red sleeveless T-shirt, *Bug Me at your Own Risk*, caught my eye. A fish tattoo on her upper arm seemed to breathe.

"Hurry up, hon, you'll miss him."

My stride lengthened. Looking down, I shaded my eyes from the sun's rays. My arm brushed Rose's shoulder A rustic, wooden skiff was tied to the end of the dock. A man with white hair leaned over the stern, pointing toward the water.

"A manatee." Rose's voice was a hoarse whisper. "See the swirl?"

I placed my left hand on the rough wood and leaned forward, craning to see the animal.

"See! There! He's a giant."

"Ah, yes. I see him."

"Manatees are endangered." Rose hunkered down. "Boat propellers are their worst enemies." She peeked over her shoulder, grinned a broad grin at the man out of earshot on her left in the boat, then lowered her voice. "Hon, I have something I want to discuss with you."

"Yeah?"

"I can't tell you here. Come to my place tonight at midnight, but don't let anyone know you're coming. Oh, and don't forget to bring the name of that clinic."

The manatee slipped below the water but came up again, this time closer to the dock. Rose and I were bent over, shoulders touching. The door behind us opened and Lil walked out.

Rose raised her voice. "Will told us once you had a thing for manatees. Isn't that right, Lil?"

I nodded. "My mom was pregnant with me when she was visiting Florida. Her bro had taken her out on a boat. They were anchored and she was lying out on the front and guess what? A big old manatee startled her with a whoosh. I guess I've heard that story so many times, manatees have become like some animal relative or something."

Rose and Lil gave each other a look.

Lil came near, gazing over the dock. "We told Will a Calusa legend about a manatee known to guard the underground temple in the Matlacha Pass. The manatee saved the temple treasure, a golden shell belonging to the Goddess of Hope by covering it with her immense body. If you protected the shell and returned it to its rightful place, it meant you would get your heart's desire. Legend has it the same manatee lives in the pass." She laughed, but neither Rose nor I joined in.

All I could think of was Will being impressed by my connection to manatees. What I saw was Will's sweet face as he heard that legend. I reached toward the water, but the manatee was gone. "Did Will stop into Bert's the night…it happened?"

Rose shot me a look. "If he did, I didn't see him. You can't imagine how many times I wished he had. I know I could have given him comforting words from our Lord and he would be alive now."

Taco, who was carrying plates of food to the table behind us, hesitated and corrected Rose. "But you went home early. Remember you were sick. They called me at home to come in, but I couldn't." Taco didn't wait for a response. Customers were waiting.

Rose grimaced. "Oh, she's right. I did go home early. God, I must be getting Alzheimer's."

Lil chimed in. "And I was in Fort Myers at my Laughter Yoga class, then I went for a Chinese meal with my instructor." Having set her alibi, she did an about-face and went inside.

Rose stepped closer. "You know, in the legend, the manatee never wanted to leave. That was her heart's desire—to remain in Matlacha forever." I stirred the water while she talked. "Of course, she gets to live forever, but, hey, it's a legend, right?"

The animal surfaced again and then vanished.

"Midnight. Tonight. Don't forget," Rose said in a conspirator's tone. "Oh, and one more thing, I don't believe in reincarnation, it's not a Christian notion. But if I did, I just might think I was a manatee myself once and maybe a pelican another time. But, I don't believe in that concept, of course."

I knew informing Rose that the doctrine of reincarnation was once part of Christianity before Catholic church leaders in Constantinople decided to delete it; that it was referred to in the Bible, both in the third and ninth chapter of John, the ninth chapter of Matthew and in the thirtieth chapter of Revelations, to name a few places—would fall on deaf ears. I merely shrugged and said, "Of course not."

Rose, a woman who had risen to the level of prime suspect

wanted to have a secret meeting. Rose had heard Will giving advice on finding an abortion clinic. She also knew he was pro-abortion. Hatred could have made her murder such a guy. Great, just great. Come alone. Tell no one. Just great.

A man walked in the door, and for a brief moment I thought. I was sure... The room slipped away as my mind slowed, darkened and twisted, then like a long ago motorcycle ride, my brain sped down a narrow path at a death defying speed...Until..." Oh!" My eyes popped open and I forced the tears back.

"Hey, you okay?" Taco was at my elbow. Her eyebrows were furrowed.

"It's nothing."

"Nothin`? It doesn't look like nothin` is bothering you." Her words drifted away. Then she added, "You look scared. You should go back home. What's keeping you down here anyways?"

I didn't, couldn't, wouldn't answer. Instead, I slipped out the back still riding that emotional motorcycle, taking the corners at such a pace it would make any thrill-seeker scream.

13

No amount of skillful invention can replace the essential element of imagination.

~ Edward Hopper

Not wanting to be alone in my room, or even go to my door, especially not near those letters that smelled of Will's cologne I sat on the motel's narrow dock on an intensely yellow Adirondack chair and sketched. The water was dark, menacing, foreboding. No moon beam created a sparkling pathway. No stars twinkled. I heard no laughter, no music coming from Bert's. Down the dock, a rat scurried up a piling. Something rancid floated by. I rubbed my neck and then realized the back of my hairline itched. Remaining still, I scanned the pass, assuming fishermen were close, but there were no boats. No fishermen or women on the bridge. I licked my lips and let my eyes roam, anticipating Lil or Rose would walk down the dock—but no one appeared. Skittish. That's the right word for how I was feeling.

It was 11:30. I was to be at Rose's at midnight. I stared out over the rippling, shadowy, sinister water. Knowing I shouldn't go, but knowing I would.

When my monkey ringtone sounded, I jumped.

Menaced by the feeling I was being watched, I pushed out of the chair, walked around the corner and went down the narrow passage to my door. "Hello!" I said into my phone way too loud.

Eyes wide, grabbing my chest, I stumbled backward. "Oh my God!" The phone crashed onto the damp planks and skidded toward a piling where it lay still.

The window to my room was shattered. Shards of glass covered the wooden planks.

I shot a glance right, left. No one.

Unlocking the door, I stepped inside. My rolled, unused canvas lay on the floor. Ripped. Defiled. I turned to the far wall where I had leaned the pelican painting. Undisturbed. Gar? Safe. Will's letters? Intact.

 I ran outside, retrieved my phone and called the cops and then Hawk. It was 3 a.m. when they drove away with their report.

Hawk assured me he would arrive in the morning, and morning couldn't come too soon.

Feeling vulnerable and violated even in the new room the motel manager helped me to move into, I was agitated. I couldn't sleep. At 7 a.m. as I was dressing to go for my walk, running footsteps made me grab Gar as quick knocks sounded on the door. Rose. My neck muscles relaxed. I let her in.

"Oh, hon, I just heard what happened. Are you all right? I saw the cop car cruising back and forth and stopped it. They told me. Oh, dear! I called Lil, but she didn't answer the phone. When I knocked on her door I found a note saying she'd be gone for a few days. It isn't like her to leave without telling me. Things are getting scary around here."

I put Gar on the nightstand and tied my last shoe lace.

Rose settled on one of the two chairs in the room. "When you didn't show last night, I thought you'd probably gone to bed early. I heard you weren't feeling so good when you left Bert's. Listen girl I'm worried and not only about your emotional state; this vandalism is a warning."

I blanched and straightened. "A warning?"

"Yeah. Someone is trying to scare you away. As much as I like you and want you to stay, go home. Hon, this place is full of poisonous snakes in disguise. You need to be careful who you anger. It wasn't that long ago Matlacha was a murderous, shoot-em-up hangout for criminals."

I stepped outside and Rose followed. A mullet leaped into the air and hit the water with a loud splash. Two kayakers paddled toward the sun. I shaded my eyes with my hand. "Why would anyone want to scare me away? I'm harmless."

"I don't know why, but you must have done something. Hon, this island paradise can be real dangerous." Everything about Rose's body language was tense. She rubbed her neck. "Hon, you should go home," she repeated, making me even more nervous.

Our eyes locked. "Why did you want me to come to your place last night, Rose?"

Rose glanced toward the entrance to the dock. "Oh, that? I was planning to read from the Bible and help you find Jesus. But, well, maybe someone is telling you that you should do that from up north and not down here."

My eyebrows went up. "That was it? Find Jesus? Why at midnight?"

Rose blushed. "Bill was visiting. He always leaves just before midnight. Come on, girl, you've had a shock. You'll think different after your run. I'm sure you've got friends at home who can help you through this mourning period. By the way, the name of that clinic?"

I knew when enough was enough. "Oh, that. It was a false alarm. My friend isn't pregnant," I said. "Just who do you think is behind this, Rose? And why do you think someone would want me to leave? Because I have no idea."

Would she believe me?

Rose bit her lip before speaking. "Of course I don't know that. I couldn't know who or why, but what happened to your room is a warning. That I'm sure of." Rose started to say something else, but apparently she changed her mind. Instead, she gave me a quick hug and hurried away.

I returned inside with Gar feeling fearful, my heart buzzing. Scoops of scare attacked my stomach. There was a very good chance I'd been seen leaving the house where I'd been spying. I might never know what had happened when the cops arrived, but I sure did know now that someone wanted to scare me into leaving. And Rose seemed to be more than aware too.

I inspected the damaged canvas, thankful that the abstract pelican painting was unscathed.

Later today I would tell Hawk about the meeting, Rose's involvement and my own fears that I was being threatened by the Army of God. He would berate me and tell me to contact the sheriff, something I should most likely do right now. But something kept me from picking up my smartphone. I wasn't sure what. Maybe just the fact that I was positive the sheriff would think me a hayseed dingbat with too active an imagination. Instead, I went to the small table in front of the curtain-covered window in view of the pass and leafed through the stack of cards filled with my notes.

Putting Rose and the anti-abortion motive aside for now, instinct told me that Will had found buried treasure. I couldn't get the idea out of my mind that Will had given someone or hidden somewhere a second map and perhaps his log. But where?

Before Hawk arrived, I'd go to the spiritual center and ask some questions and see if I could get on Demere Key.

Those would be Will-type places to leave his map and log.

14

Art happens—no hovel is safe from it, no prince may depend upon it, the vastest intelligence cannot bring it about.
~ James Abbott McNeill Whistler

Still feeling violated from the vandalism of my room, after my walk and breakfast, I drove to Pine Island Center. I turned south on Stringfellow Road and a couple miles south, went right onto Maria Drive. I parked near a white picket fence, noticing a 'Closed' sign hung on the door of the shop. Leaving my car, I went to the door and knocked, but nobody answered. The shop was closed on Fridays. Bad luck. I should have phoned ahead. Absently, I reached for my cell phone. My pocket was empty. I walked around the building.

I felt my spirits rise as I wandered the meandering paths, passing various gurgling fountains, a gazebo, fire pit, metal sculptures, pots of native plants and shaded spots with tables and chairs. I could imagine Will sitting on the bench by the small pond flanked on one side by a massive line of bamboo, reading. He would have loved this place. I thought it was pretty rad myself.

Will had been a sound believer in the idea of ley lines--the meeting points of unlike underground water sources that created highly charged and volatile currents—confused waters. According to him, Stonehenge and many medieval cathedrals and churches were built on ground above such points. Seeing and feeling the atmosphere of this peaceful setting made me have an inkling of why he held such beliefs. It wouldn't surprise me to know that there was a confused water point below these grounds. The place oozed spirituality. But no one was about. I circled the building but found no one.

Folding myself into my car, finding no phone on the seat or in the console, I realized that I'd left it back in the room. I also hadn't bothered to check for messages after my walk. Not like me. Hopefully, Hawk hadn't had any trouble catching his flight.

I steered my car in the opposite direction of Stringfellow. Having used the Florida map I'd put in the car, I knew that Demere Key was located down this gravel road. I came to a gate leading to a commercial dock and a sign that said the ramp was open to the public only on weekends. I drove through and soon entered a parking area where men were unloading metal trash bins from a barge.

To the right of where I parked was a waste disposal enclosure for Captiva and Useppa Islands` bins. Another worker was standing near a restroom and a small building. Putting on my sunglasses, I tipped my cap and stepped out onto the gravel.

Walking toward the office I approached a way skinny attendant, and showed him Will's picture. He said he recognized the man, but that he had never seen him with a metal detector. In fact, he assured me, the present owners of the property would never have allowed a private treasure hunter to explore the island. They were, he said, introverts who only worked with state and federal archeologists to uncover Calusa history and artifacts. "See that "No Trespassing" sign attached to that wire fence? It means "Keep Out." He refused to tell me the owner's name.

I thanked him. As I approached the entrance to the causeway leading to Demere Key, a golf cart driven by a woman in a floppy sun hat came to a stop. I moved her way. "Hi," I said. "Beautiful day."

The woman snatched a look at me under the hat brim, but did not stop unloading the cart of potted plants or reply.

"Oh, tomato plants," I said, hoping to get a reply. "I have a garden back home."

"Where's that?" the woman asked without looking at me.

I took a step forward. The woman's head turned quickly. I stayed where I was. "Massachusetts."

"Hm," the woman said, continuing to unload.

I introduced myself, but the woman gave only her first name, Margaret. Working hard at opening a conversation, I asked if it were true there was a house made out of shells on the island. The woman nodded, but offered no further information. I asked if the woman would mind looking at a picture to see if she could identify the man.

Setting down a pot, Margaret stepped forward, stopping short of the "No Trespassing" sign. I showed her Will's photo. The woman pursed her lips before speaking. "Oh, him! The fellow who shot himself. Sure. He came here the very morning of his death with that dreadful judge's wife—I can't remember her name, but for some strange reason that man thought by bringing her it would help him get onto my land. Humph! I guess I included her once in an invitation I sent out for an Open House. Well, I guess he learned different fast enough. That woman is a piece of work, I can tell you."

I was mystified. This didn't sound like Will.

Margaret hardly took a breath before continuing. "That woman was the one who convinced my cook's daughter to become one of her so-called clients. Clients, my foot! The woman is a pimp if you ask me and you can bet I told her that. She takes those poor girls' money, fills them full of hogwash and sets them up with old men who don't know how to treat a woman. My friend's daughter was raped by one of that woman's referrals. Of course she wouldn't file charges. She didn't want the embarrassment. I told that man and woman to get off my property and not look back! Then the next day I read about his death in *The Eagle*. A shame, but he should have been more careful who he was befriending. A person with a better heart might have been able to talk him out of it."

"But Will would never…"

"Anyone, and I mean anyone, who associates with that woman is evil." Abruptly, she returned to the cart, got in and drove back the way she had come.

I patted my breast pocket, but then remembered I was without my phone. I wanted to speak to that lying Esther Lakewood. I hurried to my car. Passing the spiritual center I noticed it still seemed quiet. I would come back when it was open. As I drove north, the sun disappeared, the wind picked up and it began to rain. I switched on the windshield wipers and as I lessened the pressure on the gas pedal, remembered the warning of last night. I changed my mind about a surprise visit to the Lakewood house. It would be wiser to talk to Esther with Hawk present. At Pine Island Center I turned right and headed for Matlacha.

Minutes later, feeling a desire to be around a friendly person whom I didn't suspect of murder, I parked in front of Luke's gallery. But pangs of violation and anger pricked my heart. I pressed my fingers together and told myself to ignore them, but that was easier said than done. Hawk would be here soon. It was ten o'clock, an hour before he was scheduled to arrive at the Fort Myers airport. I was so very, very glad of that.

Protecting my head against the driving rain with a newspaper I'd left in the car, I got out and ran for the entrance to the gallery. Wiping my feet on a floor mat and dropping the wet newspaper on the counter, I went through the door. Luke glanced my way, dropped the cloth he was using to dust onto a table and rushed forward.

"Hey, there." He took my hands in his. "Are you okay?"

The last time I'd felt so vulnerable was when I was told the news about Will. "I've felt better," I said, sighing.

"Oh, dear, I heard what happened. It's so disgusting. I'm sure it was teenagers playing a prank."

"That's what the cops say," I said. "Some prank." I kept what Rose speculated and what I'd just learned about Esther to myself.

"What was destroyed?" he asked.

"Luckily, only my roll of unused canvas and the window, of course."

His expression visibly relaxed. "Oh, I'm glad. I was worried it was your painting. Come to my place. I have the most delicious coffee brewing, and then we'll go see your work-in-progress. Creative Coast Weekend begins Friday."

I looked at his wall clock. Hawk was renting a car at the airport. It would take him about forty minutes if traffic was light to get to Matlacha. I'd arranged for him to stay in the only room left at the motel I was staying at. "I'd like that," I told him.

Luke opened an umbrella and we trotted across the road through the steady downfall.

Luke lived in a two-story house opposite the gallery. The landscaping gave the appearance that it had been planted by a landscape architect and was taken care of by a gardener.

I peered up at him as he dropped the umbrella into a stand and asked, "So, do you own another gallery besides this one?"

"Oh, yes. My original one is in Bokeelia. When I first came down here, I bought a few acres there with a house on it. I turned the house into a gallery. Once I moved to Matlacha, I hired a woman to manage it. I have another one on Sanibel. It's the moneymaker, but I prefer to live in Matlacha." He held the door open and I followed him inside.

Momentarily, I was taken aback by the fact he owned property in Bokeelia. But I liked Luke too much to put him on the suspect list, which of course is any investigator's Achilles heel.

The living room resembled my idea of an upscale decorator's dreamscape, complete with a baby grand piano. Large squares of white floor tile. High, vaulted, beaded ceiling with a fan on a long rod, whirling. Light cream-colored walls. Overstuffed, comfy furniture that begged for you to sit. Live plants and genuine artwork everywhere. I slipped out of my wet shoes and didn't hide my amazement and admiration. "My! How stunning!" I said.

He chuckled. "One of the problems with selling beautiful pieces of art is that you want to surround yourself with quality where you live. It's a gallery owner's dilemma. Make yourself at home. I'll be right back," he said, walking out of the room.

I nestled into an overstuffed chair upholstered in cream-colored cotton fabric screen-printed with feathery palm fronds. Even for an owner of three galleries, these surroundings seemed too high end. Of course, he could have inherited money. Luke walked back into the room holding two cups.

We chatted for a while before I asked, "From Will's letter I got the feeling he trusted you. Do you think he confided in you?" I tucked my legs under my body.

He sighed, sat on the sofa and stretched out his long, muscular legs, apparently a habit he had. "I always had the feeling he had something he wanted to tell me. More than once I thought he'd say it. But he never did."

I hesitated. "His dream was to discover something that would make a difference in history. That's what his treasure hunting was all about, making a difference. Sometimes he feared if he spoke of it, the dream would disappear. Maybe that's what you were feeling."

Luke cleared his throat. "Yes, perhaps. I heard he had a problem with severe depression. If you don't mind my asking, what usually triggered it?"

"An unexpected shock or disappointment."

Luke sipped his coffee. Rain tapped on the skylights.

I continued to talk. "His dad committed suicide when Will was only fifteen. Everyone thought his father was happy and content with his practice—he was a doctor in Miami where Will was raised, but one night he pulled his car up to his office and put a hose through the window. Will found him slumped over his desk."

"God, that's tough."

"Yes, well, I guess he never got over it. His dad was only

forty-six and he and his mother had just returned from a sailing trip in the Caribbean. It was the pure shock of it, the fact that he had not suspected a problem. His mother would never admit knowing his dad was depressed."

"Many people can't face the truth."

"According to Will, the Rolins family had a history of depression—emphasis on obsessive behavior. It was in the genes. Will's uncle was on lithium, but his father, who should have been medicated, refused to take medication and his mother wouldn't discuss the condition at all. Will always claimed he viewed his father's suicide in a positive light. He said if it weren't for the suicide, he would not have had the opportunity to live the type of life that suited him. His father had set up a trust fund that kicked in the year Will turned twenty-one."

"So, Will followed in his father's footsteps?"

The words, with the possibility of their ring of truth, left me speechless.

Later Luke approved my work and agreed to show the painting. He said it might be a bit too abstract for most of his customers, but he was confident that someone would recognize its true artistry. All my work began with a real life object, whether a bird, a face, a landscape or an animal, but evolved until the subject and its heart revealed itself. Once I got the inspiration from life, I never knew what the resulting painting would be. My sketches were usually realistic. But once I picked up my paint brush and faced a canvas, I never knew what would happen. Most would not recognize that this painting had begun as a pelican. But the human eyes were distinct.

When Luke left, I headed back to the motel, pulling my cellphone out of my pocket. There were two voicemails, both from Hawk asking me to phone him. I called and he answered on the first ring.

"Hi, it's me." I blew out a puff of air.

"I thought you'd never call. I figured you didn't take your phone with you. I've got terrible news. It's…it's…"

I braced myself. Grandma Murphy? His wife? "What is it?" I asked in a whisper.

"It's my son. He…" Hawk's voice broke into a sob.

I stopped and leaned against the bridge railing. "What happened?"

"We're at the hospital now. He's, he's had a stroke."

"My God! At two and a half?"

"I know. It's unbelievable. Hey, there's the doc. I need to run. Will you be okay?"

Who, little old me?

"Of course. The cops caught the teens who vandalized my room. In fact, it's starting to look like Will did end his own life," I lied. "Don't worry about me. I'll call later. Give my love to Lia and Jamie. If there's anything I can do, anything at all, please let me know. Hawk, I'm so sorry."

I pocketed my phone and walked on. Poor Hawk and Lia. I withdrew my phone, clicked on a saved contact and ordered a bouquet of balloons to be sent to the hospital. I knew that's where they would have taken Jamie. I'd leave right after the show. Hopefully, by then I'd be able to call the sheriff with concrete news that would make him reopen the investigation.

Hawk would be engrossed by this tragedy for several weeks. I could not count on him for help. As his friend, I needed to head home soon so I could be support. Opening my motel room door, I focused on Gar and shut the door. I went to the night stand, picked up my note cards and sat close to Gar, my bud.

Rose's card was first. I read it to Gar. "At this point, Rose—a devout anti-pro-lifer is the prime suspect with a motive because Will helped one of Taco's friends (or was it her?) find a clinic for an abortion and she overheard him doing it. Her alibi is that she was working at Bert's, but Taco said she had left early, so that alibi is non-existent. She also attempted to get me to come to her place in the early morning hours alone, warning me to tell no one. Her motherly mask could be cover for a religious fanatic who is a killer." I stared at Gar. "Bottom line, I'll never, never be alone in a private place with

Rose again and I'll keep my guard up when she's around. She should be arrested soon. The cops can question her about Will's murder."

Card two: The judge. "Did the judge kill Will out of jealous rage? His alibi, and his wife's, was that they'd been together at the Barbara Mann show and dinner afterward which checked out. Paid off the waiter?" I put down the cards and opened a water bottle. "Well, that seems a stretch, doesn't it Gar? As much I don't like him, I don't think he did it."

Card three: Esther. "Liar. Victimizer of young women. Lied about being with Will the day he died. It had to be after he was seen with Taco. Did Esther kill Will because Will was going to expose her business as some kind of crude escort service? Evil woman. If it wasn't Rose, it might be her."

I placed Esther's card under Rose's and set the judge's aside.

Jay Mann's card was fourth and I read it outloud with emphasis. "Was what Will and Jay fought about serious enough for Jay to murder Will? Where was he the night Will was killed? Is he somehow involved in illegal activity connected to treasure? Is he the seeder (if there is one) that Gator spoke of?"

I stopped and took a drink of water before reading further. "If Will did learn a seeder's identity, he would definitely inform the authorities. If Jay learned he was planning to do this, he might kill him to keep his mouth shut. Possible?" I glared at Gar. "Stop worrying. I won't allow my sympathy for him to color my judgment. His story could be an out and out lie. Okay, Gar, I need to ask Jay why he was so upset about the party, and see if I can get him to open up about any possible interest he might have in treasure hunting, especially sunken ships."

I slid his card under Esther's.

Card Five: "Taco. Helped a friend get an abortion. Was it Margaret's cook's daughter? Alibi: With parents. Easy to check. No motive yet. Will and she seemed to have been friends of sorts. Will, like he often did, tried to protect a friend.

Nothing new there. That certainly would not be a reason for Taco to kill him, right? I just don't think it was her."

The card went on top of the judge's. I took another swallow.

Card Six: "Lil. If Will found treasure and told Lil and she needed the money, does she have it in her to kill for it? Seemed so. She did almost lose her Bokeelia land. Will said he was digging in Bokeelia. She did recently pay off that debt. Motive: greed and need. Alibi: Said she was at a yoga class in Fort Myers and dinner with the teacher. An easy thing to check."

I lowered the card. "But Lil couldn't have had time to get rid of gold or jewelry that was hundreds of years old fast enough to pay off that bill. Unless she was a master and well connected thief, and that she surely is not."

I set Lil's card on top of Taco's.

When I was done, I had confused myself so thoroughly I started sorting all over again.

But I knew who my chief suspects were now: Rose, Esther and Jay Mann.

15

Emotion can't be added on, nor imitated. It is the bud. The work of art is the budding.

~ *Georges Braque*

Now that Hawk would no longer be able to be at my side, I realized I would have to be more vigilant about my safety. Leaving my phone home yesterday was a sign that I didn't have my head in the game like I should. I was tempted to stop at Luke's and spill the can of garbanzo beans about my real reason for being in Matlacha and all that had happened since I'd arrived, but decided not to. As much as I wished for a real live sidekick I could trust who could help watch my back, I cautioned myself against this action. I'd been on the islands one week and already many people seemed more like chameleons than anything else. Luke, too, could be someone other than I thought he was. I'd keep my own counsel and make sure I had my phone with me at all times. I would not meet anyone in private and keep an eye out to make sure I wasn't being followed. If things began to feel too dangerous, I'd contact the sheriff. Surely I could trust him.

While finishing my second cup of java, I phoned Esther Lakewood. Esther agreed to meet me at ten at the deli in Pine

Island Center. My plan was to confront her with what I'd learned to see what Esther's explanation would be. I would then go to the spiritual center to talk to the owners.

It was a breezy seventy-five degree morning. The sky was blanketed in clouds that drifted across the mangroves as I drove my car westward. Hawk's son's situation wasn't far from my mind.

Esther wasn't there when I arrived. I ordered my third cup of coffee of the morning and a Danish, then went back outside to sit under an umbrella. A couple eating breakfast nodded at me and I returned the greeting as Esther pulled up in a silver Porsche. As Esther exited the car, she waved gaily at me.

Esther was dressed in a sleeveless V-neck sundress and beaded flip flops. A turquoise cotton hat covered her hair. Large tortoise sunglasses hid her eyes. She bounced up the steps and sat, smiling broadly—relaxed, shining; ready for the world to appreciate her beauty and charm.

I hated to burst the woman's fake Pollyanna bubble so soon, but I wasn't in the mood for pleasantries. As soon as Esther sat, I pulled off my sunglasses, so that Esther could see my eyes. Intertwining my fingers, I placed them on the table.

Esther grinned at a man walking by before she gave me her attention. When she saw my solemn, no nonsense expression, she sobered and recoiled, as if she'd seen a snake.

Or did I just associate snakes with her?

I hope my tone of hurt and disappointment added impact to my opening words. "I'm really, really upset with you. I asked for your help during my grieving process and what do I get? Lies."

Taken aback, Esther blinked fast. "My dear, whatever are you talking about?" She looked about as innocent as a Crocodile heading for a chicken.

"You told me you'd only seen Will twice. Once when you met him and then the night he asked you to give back Taco's money."

"Yes. That's right. So?" Esther was now inspecting her manicured fingernails.

"I just had a talk with the owner of Demere Key," I said in my flattest, most accusatory voice.

Esther didn't bat a fake eyelash, but her tone hardened ever so slightly. "You talked to Margaret? Well, my, my! You do get around, don't you?" She shrugged. "I went with Will to introduce him to the family. So what? It was my way of showing him I wasn't the bad person he thought I was." She hesitated, readjusting herself in her chair.

I wondered if Esther were waiting to see if I would correct her. I didn't.

Esther continued. "Unfortunately, Margaret was in a bad mood. She refused to welcome Will as a guest. I felt sorry for him. He so wanted to explore that island."

No mention of the rape or Esther's part in the crime.

"Why didn't you mention this before?"

Esther let out a dramatic puff of air.

Like, make me gag.

"My dear, I see I made a mistake. I know you're in mourning. I certainly didn't think it would help you to know that your lover was shunned on the day he died. But I see now I was wrong. I apologize. Will was terribly, terribly disappointed and embarrassed by the rejection. He took it far too personally. I can see now that by telling you this earlier it would have helped you understand his state of mind on the day he, well, he died. Suicide is so hard to understand."

Esther couldn't know that I was aware, according to other accounts that Will was in a particularly good mood on the day of his death. With a concerted effort, I allowed Esther to believe that Margaret hadn't told me about accusing her of being a pimp. It hadn't been Will who had been rejected. It had been Esther. And Will would have known that. Letting Esther pat my hand, I lowered my head and asked, "So *that* was the last time you saw Will?"

"Yes, my dear, the last and the only other time. I'm so sorry. I should have been more upfront with you. It's so hard to know what to say to a person in mourning."

I was already zeroing in on how I could find out the last

name of the rape victim. Taco, of course.

Shortly after, we parted and anyone who saw us hugging would have thought we were the best of friends.

Keeping an eye on the rearview mirror, I turned the car down Maria Drive, heading for the spiritual center.

After parking I walked through the front door, stopping at the counter to the left. The woman tending was no stranger. I had previously questioned her about Will at Bert's. I asked her if the owners were around and she said they were out back preparing for a wedding. I was surprised when the woman added, "I believe they've been expecting you."

A second woman with frosted blonde hair wearing a sleeveless green sundress was directing the preparations. Chairs and tables were being set up under a long open-air structure. The gazebo was being draped in fabric. A husky man in a cap walked toward me, extending his hand. "Welcome," he said, "you've come back."

I assumed he thought I was with the wedding party; probably a sister of the bride come to check on the arrangements, but I soon found I was mistaken. He and his wife actually did know who I was. And, yes, they did seem to be expecting me. "But we've never met!" I said.

The man who introduced himself as James and his wife as Nancy gestured for me to take a seat on a bench facing a labyrinth. Before we could speak again, Nancy joined us. She was a sweet-faced woman who made me feel even more comfortable in this spiritual place. "Don't think we're psychic. We live over there." She motioned toward a two-story structure beyond a grove of trees. I had not noticed the house on my previous brief visit.

"We saw you and tried to catch you, but you were too quick for us. We asked around. It wasn't hard to find out who you were. We knew you'd return and if you hadn't once the wedding preparations were in place, we would have sought you out."

James added, "We have something for you that Will left in our safekeeping. He told us not to give it to anyone except a woman named Jessie Murphy."

I was amazed and told them so. James stood and strolled toward the house. Nancy told me how much they liked Will. He had spent hours with them sharing his excitement over his hunt for treasure. They were particularly impressed with how he wasn't interested in the possibility of becoming rich or famous. The process and desire to uncover something of historical significance—the giving back, he said was of chief importance to him. As stewards of the earth, their philosophies were similar. "We were devastated when we heard of his death," she added.

James was standing in front of us now with an envelope in his hand. With a reverent motion, he passed it to me and took a step backward. Tears welled up in my throat. My heart tripped over itself. Will had left something for me. It was not big enough to be a folded map and not thick or heavy enough to be a log. All I could think was that this could be a sure sign he did commit suicide. I was heartsick.

"I can't thank you enough," I said, holding it to my chest, but fearing what this might mean.

James raised his hand. "Please. Words aren't necessary."

Moments later rounding the car, I opened the driver's door and slid behind the wheel, breathless, distraught.

Did I really want to read his last thoughts? Would they make me feel even more guilt?

Unconsciously tapping on the steering wheel I reopened the door. Ducking my head, I went around the east side of the building. Everyone was busy with the preparations. No one stopped me to talk. I sat on the same bench to the left of the pond, two feet from the labyrinth. The trees behind the pond's shore cast long shadows. A turtle moved toward the water and dropped in. I didn't hear the splash. A heron landed near the distant, towering bamboo. Its wings hugged its regal body. I tore off the end of the envelope and took out the sheet of paper and words leapt off the page at me:

November 18th.

Dear Weiner,

If you're reading this (and I hope you won't have to), it means I'm no longer a part of this planet. My soul is soaring, longing for a new body to enter. I also know what you're doing. You're busying yourself investigating my demise. You be careful, girl. People aren't who you think they are.

I've written a goofy poem that contains a riddle meant only for you. I know. I know. You hate puzzles. But to tell you the truth, I don't trust anyone anymore. A shame, huh? I think the economy has made people do things they'd normally never do.

Listen, Wiener, I will always love you, but when this is all over I want you to find someone to take my place. Make it someone who will respect you as a painter. You're so talented. Fill up the world with your work.

Paint and sketch, my sweetheart. The Universe has given you a gift. Don't let that gift go to waste.

So, here's the goofy riddle. Read and remember.

Pirate Story

Two of us afloat near the mangrove in the pass
Two of us making love encircled by sea grass
Winds in the air, blowing wild,
And waves on the shore bite like a naughty child
Where shall we venture, today that we're afloat?
Wary of the weather but steering the boat
Shall it be to Sanibel, across the bay
To Pine Island, Demere Key, or Matlacha?
Ha! But here's a guide playing in the Gulf
A dolphin before us, do not scoff
Quick, don't let him escape; he's as smart as can be,
Taking you to a place where love will always be.

Oh, Will…Will…Will…

Tears flowed down my face. I knew the place. How could I ever forget? It was where I had my first time, my very first time. And Will was so gentle, so concerned. And when we were done, we laughed until we both cried.

Pushing myself up from the bench, I stumbled into the single-path labyrinth. Head down, I encircled the stone maze, angry, confused, and devastated. But something made me continue. And gradually, ever so slowly, I felt my spirit leave the world of the labyrinth and sink below the roots of the bamboo, burrow into the sludge at the bottom of the pond. It was as if I had meditated without intending to do so, and when I reached the beginning again, I was at peace. Ready to return to the place I was sure Will's riddle wanted me to go to. It was clear to me that he had buried the log there and most likely his map as well. He'd written a riddle that no one but me would understand. I shuddered at the thought of gentle Will believing, even perhaps knowing, he was the target of a killer.

Stepping out of the kayak I had rented into foot-deep water, I pulled the boat toward shore and tied it to a log on the beach, the same log I had used the day Will had brought me here. The beach was no longer than twenty feet and less than five feet wide.

Raising my chin I let the sun's rays warm my throat and face. Think positive thoughts, not negative. Draw positive energy towards you. Will had taught me this. You cannot think negative and positive thoughts at the same time. Choose the positive. I gave one quick nod and holding onto my flip flops, I sloshed onto shore. I loved sand between my toes, even sand that was peppered with sharp twigs and edges of seashells.

I headed straight for the encircling mangrove. "Surely he buried them," I mumbled. I combed the edge of the thick foliage, but found no hint of where that might be.

I lightly kicked a piece of driftwood and turned it over, but no note. On that day, Will had torn off the label of the water bottle we'd been sharing and taking a pen from his pocket, he had written: *Will loves Jessie. Jessie loves Will.* Then childishly he had buried it by a rock. Our love, he said, was now a part of this isolated island.

The rock. Of course.

I looked around and frowned. No rock. It had been close to the shore.

Heading toward the kayak, I carefully moved aside several branches of mangrove. I smiled. The top of a rock was barely visible. But it was the rock. I was sure of it.

Getting down on my knees and using my hands, I began to dig. Sand flew everywhere. Until, bingo, my fingers scratched across something metal.

Sitting, I scooped up an elongated box, dusted off the remaining wet sand and opened it. And there they were—the folded map and his black leather bound log. I flipped to the last entry and facing the bay, read:

I woke up this morning at 4 a.m. wired. Something was in the air—an energy that kept my nerve endings sizzling. I could feel it. It was like no other feeling I'd ever had before. Once Jessie said when she's painting and knows it's good, it's like being in a zone. Well, that's it. Being in a zone. I couldn't even eat any breakfast, I was that excited. I was in Bokeelia at the site by sunrise. All I could think about was that I wished Jessie were here to share this moment. Every time I tossed another shovel of sand my heart pounded louder. So by the time my shovel hit the chest, well, I was hardly even surprised. That's how sure I was that it would be there.

Last evening I went to the spiritual center to meditate and leave her a note before going for my nightly swim. During the meditation I saw bright colored shapes fitting together, separating, and then fitting together again. They were the most vivid colors I've ever seen in my inner life and it was when the session was over that I realized success was so near. A glow came over me and would not go away. Even now, as I write this, though the glow is gone, I remember it. Perhaps I always will.

The chest is here with me in my room safely out of sight until tomorrow when I'll call the historic society. Selfishly, I wanted to be alone with it at least for a bit. It's just so unbelievable to see it.

I find it difficult to touch the coins or the jewels, touching might take away the magic. Magic, perhaps, is not something to hold in your hand.

Some would take photos I guess. That will happen. But I won't be the photographer. How can you capture your dream in a digital box?

I lowered the letter and blinked rapidly. Oh, Will. You *were* depressed.

I almost called Jessie today. The urge to share with her was so strong, almost overwhelming, but that would be breaking a promise and I won't do that.

This is the last log entry. I think my treasure hunting days are over. How can you top fulfilling your dream? Why would you want to try?

There are those who would do evil to have what I have discovered, but if that happens, even they cannot take this moment from me.

But I'm taking precautions. The poem for Jessie. Burying this log and map. And something that will surprise anyone who knows me—especially Weiner—I've loaded dad's old gun—the one he used…and set it on my desk.

I burst into tears.

16

Art is a technique of communication. The image is the most complete technique of all communication.

~ Claes Oldenburg

Back in Matlacha I called Hawk and asked how his son was doing and found out he was still in the hospital, but stable. I knew I had phoned as much to get his report on his son as to hear his voice. It always made me feel stronger and more capable than I believed I was. I didn't tell him that Will had found buried treasure. If I did, he'd know Will had been murdered and I was in danger. He had enough to worry about. As he talked about how miraculously his son was doing, I chewed on a pencil eraser. When he was finished, I assured him I'd be home soon. I inspected the painting that would soon be put on Luke's gallery wall for exhibit—a bigger than life otherworldly winged creation with Will's eyes. A man the log proved who was murdered.

It was apparent and heart sickening that Will was killed for the contents of the chest. I didn't want to imagine what might happen if someone in financial trouble suddenly were faced with a chest of gold and an idealist who only wanted to turn it over to authorities.

From his log entry it didn't sound like he was spreading the word. But who might have found out? Rose? Esther? Jay Mann? All possibilities. I phoned the sheriff and told him about the log and map. He said he would send a deputy over immediately to retrieve them. I felt relieved. The case would be reopened. I could pack and head home, but not until after the art show. I owed myself that.

As I stood near my car at a parking space a pelican swooped low, startling me. I drew in a deep breath of salt air and headed for the door. Bert's was relatively quiet. No live music. Very few customers. I went directly to my favorite table on the back dock. A flock of black and gold birds hovered overhead, eyeing the fries on the paper plate left abandoned on the table. The bow of a boat bobbed in the dark water near the pier.

"Hey, there!"

Another boat drifted toward the pier. A man in a navy blue T-shirt and khaki shorts waved to Lil who had just come outside. A gusty wind swept across the dock. Lil tipped her head and walked down the pier as another man hopped off and tied to a piling.

"Haven't seen you for awhile," the man in the blue T-shirt called.

"Yeah," Lil said.

The robust man stepped onto the dock and wrapped his arm around Lil.

They disappeared around the corner. I could hear them chatting. Unconsciously, I tapped the pencil on the rough wood near my sketch pad.

A high-end runabout motored in through the channel. Twenty-four, twenty-five feet of pricey fiberglass—rocking and rolling in the chop. It neared the piling, motored on. I put down my pencil and cringed. "Too fast, woman, cut the engine."

A young woman stood in the stern, a line in her hand. At seeing the captain, I swallowed my surprise and stood. The engine purred. I moved fast. The bow was still too far out. The stern threatened to scrape the first boat. Snatching a metal pole that lay on the planking, I placed it against the side, making the boat turn toward the dock. Esther Lakewood cut the engine. "Thanks for coming down," she said.

Another woman tossed the line. I pulled the boat forward and tied it off.

"Pretty brave of you to be out in these seas." I eyed the three young women with Esther the Evil. Barbie dolls all.

Esther laughed as they climbed out of the boat. "Half the pleasure," she said. "My dears, I'd like to introduce you to one of Matlacha's artists, Jessie Murphy. These girls are my clients. I brought them over for the festivities. We're staying close by. Girls, shake Jessie's hand. Now make sure you take a firm grip. Wimpy handshakes promise other wimpy responses. Jessie, I hear, is showing one of her pieces in one of the galleries this weekend."

The young women giggled.

Esther smiled. "This beauty is Lucinda."

Lucinda nodded and extended her hand.

"And, the lovely, Sabrina. And, last but definitely not least, the luscious, Endira."

Sabrina was as tall as me and similar auburn hair color.

Had me by a mile for looks.

Lucinda was no more than five foot two, had blonde hair and weighed one-hundred pounds, if that. Sabrina looked like a woman who worked out too much on weights. Her biceps rippled. Her breasts were the size of bowling balls. To say Endira was luscious was an understatement. She had enlarged lips, sultry looks and a smile that promised volumes of fun. They wore various colored short shorts, sleeveless T's and their skin was oiled and bronzed. "Geez," I said, "I feel like a Hollywood movie set just arrived."

Esther beamed. "Now, girls, we won't bother Ms. Murphy." She nodded toward the sketch pad. "She's obviously working. Come. My husband is here somewhere. I know he can't wait to meet you."

In a flurry of eye-catching flesh, they swept around the

corner.

Closing my sketch pad and standing, I went inside and found a table where I could hear and view the spot where the judge sat so I could shamelessly eavesdrop on their conversation. I was surprised I hadn't noticed the judge earlier. By adjusting my body, their view of me was blocked by a post.

"Oh, there he is. Come on, girls!" Esther said.

The women situated themselves at a table with the judge. I heard the introductions, watched the smiling exchange of handshakes and waited. Esther's voice was loud. "Would you bring an umbrella over here?" Esther asked.

"But I love the sun," the blonde whined, brightening her lips with a tube of lipstick.

Esther's back straightened. "Refined women do not get too much sun, least you prematurely age your skin. And, no tanning booths."

Well, I did wear a cap and did use sun block.

The blonde hung her head, but not before giving Esther a disgruntled look.

"You're here to learn new habits, right?" Esther asked.

"But, this doesn't look like a place millionaire's come to," Lucinda said, taking in the rustic building and presenting a pout to the other women.

"Never be deceived by appearances, girls. Wealthy men who live by the sea love to frequent places like this, especially ones where you can arrive by boat. Isn't that right, Harold?"

Harold winked at the girl and tipped the bill of his captain's cap back showing his broad forehead.

Lucinda pursed her thick lips and appeared to look more appreciatively at her surroundings.

"Ladies," the new male waiter, Danny, asked. "Can I get you a drink?"

Sabrina began to speak, "I'll have a…"

With a heavy sigh, Esther interrupted by placing her hand on Sabrina's. "Even in a place like this, a lady does not order her own drinks in the presence of a gentleman of means, not even if the waiter is rude enough to directly ask you." She turned her shoulder to Danny who rolled his tongue around the inside of his mouth, bristled and turned his attention to the judge. "What can I get you and the ladies?"

"Coronas all around with lime," he said. "Today is a day to celebrate. Don't you think so, my dears?"

"Why?" Sabrina asked, batting her eyes.

"This is your very first day of class with my charming wife. It's a landmark day. You will be the first of her triumphs." He patted Esther's hand. "By the way, where is that brunette?"

Esther hugged her husband. "Thank you, Harold, Oh, and Taco…I must really find out what her real name is—such a horrible nickname…is tied up for the afternoon. She'll catch up with us later." She looked earnestly at each young woman. "We shall all welcome Taco with arms wide. In fact, Endira, I believe you already know her. Is that right?"

"Yes, Mrs. L. We've been friends since fifth grade."

"I thought so. That's even a better reason to be nice to a girl with the misfortune of being named after food. Right?"

Dutifully, they each nodded.

The waiter brought the drinks and the judge made a toast. Then he began chatting quietly with Endira who sat on his left. Casually he draped his arm over her chair. Hand touching shoulder, he leaned close to her ear and whispered.

Esther's face surged and glowed fire engine red. She shot up straighter in her chair and slammed her palm on the table so hard beer splattered over the judge's fingers. "Harold!" she exclaimed.

With an annoyed expression, his head pivoted, his lips positioned carefully in a thin line. "Esther, my dear," he said in a condescending tone, "please calm down. You're over-reacting again." He did not remove his arm, but instead, his fingers rubbed Endira's shoulder. Looking at each woman in turn, he flashed a sad-eyed look.

"Over-react! Over-react! I'll show you over-react!"

The judge appeared crestfallen. "My dear, please." Slowly, he removed his fingers, then his arm.

Outraged, Esther stood, toppling over her chair. "Come, girls. This is ridiculous."

"Esther, please!"

I saw a flash of movement toward the back door. A figure in black ducked away. Taco?

Esther's voice vibrated the salt air.

I turned my attention back to the squabbling couple.

"You're making a laughing stock of my course. Shame on you, Harold," Esther said.

She stomped toward the Grady White, followed sheepishly by the three obviously confused and bewildered young women. "Sabrina, untie that line. Come on. Get on board. Meeting with Harold was a mistake. Such an insult."

"What insult?" Lucinda asked.

I couldn't help but chuckle.

Esther's shoulders heaved. I could tell she was working hard at self-control. "Sit!" Esther finally yelled. Turning the key, she shifted into reverse and the boat left the dock so fast she clipped the corner. She did not look back. I couldn't help imagine that she was in a pointed black hat and long flowing robe riding a broom stick.

"Good lord!" Lil said, eyes twinkling. "That was quite a scene!"

"I don't think Esther likes her husband coming on to her clients," I said. I watched as the judge nonchalantly paid the bill, took a final sip of his beer and headed for the door. It seemed jealousy ran in the Lakewood family. Tit for tat or cat for rat.

Lil sat. "So?"

"The judge knew what he was doing. This is a public place. I think he deliberately made his wife jealous, knowing how she would react."

"Why would he do that?"

"Maybe he wants to show everyone how angry his wife can get." Perhaps, I thought, he wanted *me* to see that. Or did he want Taco to overhear?

"Why?"

"Good question. I don't know," I added. I was thoughtful, contemplating the meaning of the Lakewood scene as Jay Mann walked through the door. "I thought you didn't come here often?"

He shrugged.

Wiping her hands on a towel, Rose came out of the kitchen and saw me. "Are you leaving today, hon?" she asked.

I settled on the stool next to Jay who ordered coffee. "Naw, I'm in no hurry," I said. "Teenagers can't scare me away."

A flicker came and went quickly in Rose's eyes. She frowned her disapproval and walked to the end of the bar.

Jay drew his coffee mug across the tabletop and then raised it and sipped. As he lowered the mug, his eyes met mine.

Rose brought me a black coffee and without speaking, left abruptly.

Jay ran his mug back and forth across the rough wood. "I heard about the window and your break-in. That had to freak you out."

"Oh, yeah, that was Freaksville, all right. But not much was actually damaged, just some canvas." I tried to smile, but the result was less than cheerful.

"I guess you're getting a fuller picture. This isn't paradise as many would like to think."

"Ah, come on, no place is perfect. But I'm beginning to wonder why Will stayed so long. If it weren't for the treasure hunting, he would have returned home long ago. From what I've heard he argued with a lot of people down here, including you and Lil."

"Lil argue with someone? You're kidding," he said in mock surprise.

I let that pass. "So what was your beef with Will?"

Jay sipped without answering.

I put on my mask of innocence. "If you don't want to tell me about it…"

As I hoped he would, he interrupted me. "I don't mind at

all. He heard about a little project of mine and he called me a thief."

"A little project?"

"Yeap. I'm a sculptor, but few artists can make a living as such. I had the good fortune of turning a hobby of mine into a lucrative business."

"Really?"

"Yes, well, my money maker has to do with treasure—sunken treasure—from ships that went down."

Jay's frankness surprised me. This didn't sound like a man who had something to hide.

Jay continued. "I conduct the research, find the ships, get investors to invest to cover expenses like divers and cranes, etc. and bring up the loot. We split the proceeds. I've been successful twice. Once off the keys. Once in the Gulf."

"But that doesn't sound illegal," I said, watching him closely.

"Precisely. There is nothing illegal about it. But Will heard some cock-and-bull story about how there was a seeder in Matlacha bilking investors and after seeing some marine maps in my home and a couple of obvious hundred-year-old coins, he decided I was the man. Get real!"

Jay worked his shoulders back and forth. "On no concrete evidence at all, he told two men who had invested that I was a seeder. In case you don't know, that's someone who drops small bits of gold coins or an artifact or two into a sunken ship to entice and fool investors into thinking they'll get richer. I couldn't believe he was spreading such lies. I threatened to sue him for libel." He rubbed his neck and looked me squarely in the eye. "My investors bought the story and wanted out. I gave them back their money immediately. Their loss. This new find would have returned their money six-fold. It's absolutely incredible how people will believe rumors without checking them out first."

Gator's story. Yes, gullible Will. I could imagine Will going on the crusade—so Will.

"Why didn't you just give them a list of people who were

happy with their former investments? If they were smart, they could have checked out your business."

He sniffed. "I can't wait to see their faces when the story comes out in the newspaper about how much treasure we discover. This one is going to be big! I have never in my life done anything illegal. Too bad Will couldn't see that. I was disappointed in him. I thought he understood me better than that."

I believed him on his last point. It had taken me many conversations before Will understood how important it was for me to have some time alone. His obsessive nature made it difficult to get him to see another viewpoint, but once he saw it—he got it. Sort of.

But him saying he'd never done anything illegal? I wondered where he put his pot smoking in that equation. Anyone who walked into this studio unannounced had to know he smoked. His business. Not mine.

"Will wasn't perfect," I said, "but he was a good guy."

"Yes, I'm sure, just too gullible. I wish I knew who was spreading that story. I'd give them a piece of my mind. Don't worry, I don't plan to badmouth Will now that's he's…gone. But you asked."

I picked up my pencil. "So, what's the name of your business? It sounds fascinating."

Jay finished his coffee. "Mann Incorporated. I'm always looking for new investors. But, as I said, this deal is winding down. Want me to keep you in mind for any future dives?"

"Oh, sure. As if I'd have money to invest." His story would be easy to check. I was surprised Will hadn't bothered. Well, not that surprised, knowing Will wasn't exactly a computer lover. I remembered that I needed to ask where Jay was the night of Will's death. But cautioned myself to not do it directly. "There must have been quite a scene the night Will was found."

"I suppose. But I was in Sarasota with a prospective investor. When I returned I planned to show Will a contract and give him my URL so he could see I was legit, but I never got the chance."

I reminded myself that the cops would take care of the investigation from now on, but just in case, I made note of Jay's information.

Nothing was rented until the lease was signed. Absolutely nothing.

17

*Every opaque object that is devoid of color partakes of the
color of that which is opposite to it,
as happens with a white wall.*
~ Leonardo Da Vinci

The following morning the sea and town were covered in a heavy fog. I bent over to catch my breath after my power walk and was surprised when I heard a woman's voice.

"I can't believe that's good for you." Taco stood in front of the coffee house, cigarette in hand.

I slid my blue terrycloth band higher on my sweaty forehead. Taco starting a conversation with me? How interesting. "It's what keeps me sane." I swiped my chin.

"Whatever it takes."

I began my leg stretches. Whenever I did, I thought about the man who had taught me the best way to do them, my karate teacher from Shanghai. One day he had spoken of the Book of Yao and a philosophy that made perfect sense. Chia. Kuo. Pang. Ming. Cultivate self. Become an example for others. Regulate your surroundings, working toward harmony. The result would be universal accord. After that lesson, I had attempted to apply the concept to everything I did. But it wasn't easy. Old habits were hard to break. With my hand on my knee, I extended my left leg and grinned at Taco. "Do you exercise?"

"I've just started tennis lessons. They're cool."

"A suggestion by Mrs. Lakewood?" I asked, wiping my forehead.

Taco's eyes narrowed. Suspicion etched her voice. "Who told you that?"

"No one. It was a guess."

Taco's expression and body language relaxed. She tapped her cigarette on an empty flower pot by her right leg. "Oh! Well then…Yeah. Sure, why not?"

I was surprised Taco was still smoking. I would have thought that disgusting habit would have been the first one Esther would have eliminated. "Love your necklace," I said, changing positions.

Taco put her hand on the gold pendant around her neck. "Thanks. It was my grandmother's."

"Are you happy with the course?" I asked.

Taco flipped her cigarette butt into the center of the cracked ceramic pot. "Mrs. L's? What's it to you?"

"Just curious."

Taco shrugged. "She's okay. Kind of stuck up, but okay. Her husband is a jerk, but there aren't too many guys who aren't."

"He seemed chummy with your friend Endira."

"I've got her back. She knows that."

"I heard her mother is a cook for the people who own Demere Key." Taco caught my eye. "Yeah, so?" That's what I thought—the rape victim.

"She's lucky to have you for a friend."

Taco shuffled her feet. "There's something I want to tell you, something you might want to know. It's about Rose. She's not who you think she is."

Uh, huh. So someone else was aware of Rose's secret life. "What do you mean?"

"Well, she's nice and all that, but she's fanatical, if you

know what I mean."

Oh, yeah. I knew all right. I feigned innocence. "No, I don't. Could you be more specific?"

"Rose gets real weird when it comes to abortion. After you asked me if she overheard my conversation or argument with Will, I remembered something. I, ah, saw her with this guy the night Will was killed. They were near his duplex. When Rose saw me she laughed and said he was a guest of hers from out of town, but I didn't buy that. There was something about him that made me, well, wonder why he was near Will's duplex. Anyway, I have no proof or anything that he was doing anything wrong. He was just nosing around. But it was the night Will was found."

"Did you tell this to the sheriff?"

"I don't talk to that jerk."

This didn't surprise me. I didn't like to talk to him either. Not with how he treated women. "Would you recognize the man with Rose if you saw him again?"

"Maybe.

"What if I tell the sheriff what you said?"

"Sure. Fine. You do that. He knows where he can find me. Got to go. My mom's expecting me."

"So, you live at home?"

"Yeah. Can you believe it? At my age? I can't wait to finish Mrs. L's course. Luckily, I have a room where I don't have to come across my dad. I ain't spoken to him for years. The dipwad helped put my brother in jail."

"That must be hard."

"What?"

"Living in the same house with your parents."

Taco flipped her cigarette butt into a pile of pebbles. "Everything has its ups and downs. Are you happy that you let Will come down here on his own?"

Ouch. That hit home.

Without waiting for an answer, Taco circled around me and walked away.

When I got back to the room, Luke was at the door. I

nodded. "Hi, there."

He smiled. "Sorry to bother you, but I thought I'd check on your progress."

I unlocked the door and we stepped inside.

"Hey, Gar, how's it goin`?"

I pointed to the completed painting. "What do you think?"

Luke turned his head this way and that. "Unique. Enchanting. Delightful," he said. "As soon as the fog lifts I'll drive my truck down and we can transfer it." He folded his arms over his chest, continuing his inspection. "You'll help me position it, of course."

"Of course."

He strolled leisurely toward the hot plate. "May I?"

"The tea bags are in the Ball jar on the shelf."

"Right."

I studied the liquid gray eyes on the 4 x 6 foot canvas. I had planned to name the work "Wisdom." Lil teased me about the choice. Too philosophical and abstract, she said. She preferred something more concrete, like: "Endangered."

"What do you think of the title?" I asked Luke, motioning toward a sheet of paper taped to the easel.

"Well…" He pursed his lips, but said nothing else.

Impatiently, I waved him aside. "That's okay. You're not the only one who doesn't like it."

"Don't be offended. The painting is wonderful. The title? You can do better."

I shrugged. "You're probably right. I didn't get enough sleep last night, that's all."

After Luke left I chewed on the tip of a pen, then wrote: "Butternut: Truth has Wings" and signed my name, thinking: What am I going to do when all this is settled and I have all those hours alone without him?

Someone knocked on the door. A deputy. I handed over the log and map. He had me sign a release form and left.

An hour later I stood near the motel entrance waiting for Luke. I wanted to get this transfer done, so I could talk to the sheriff again in person with Taco's information. I'd already made a call and found out Jay's business was legit, so he was definitely off my suspect list. With a witness who saw Rose and a man outside Will's apartment, plus the log, the case had to be reopened. I'd like to see if I could get the sheriff to tell me anything. But even if he didn't, after Creative Coast Weekend, I planned to head back to Cambridge and let the cops find Will's killer.

"Hey, girl! Ready?" Luke slammed his truck door.

Gingerly we lifted and carried the painting to the truck for the short trip across the bridge to the gallery. We hung it on the far wall of the first room beside a mermaid in muted shades of gold, blue and silver. Promising to return later in the day, I headed across the bridge where I found Jay talking to a fisherman. When I approached, I greeted him and the fisherman dropped his line in the water.

Jay asked to join me on the walk to the motel. "There's something I haven't told you. The other night when you left Bert's someone was following you."

"Me?" My voice squeaked.

"Yeah. The dogs scared him off, but someone was following you all right. I chased him, but he got away. I stayed outside your door for quite some time."

"Him? Was it definitely a man?"

"I'm not sure. That was my assumption, but it could have been a woman."

Standing at my car I thanked him and he left. I made a quick call to make sure the sheriff would be at his office, then hopped into my car and shifted into reverse.

Sheriff Schilling was waiting for me. Neither his voice, nor his body language was friendly as he seemed to toy with balancing another unlit cigar on the ashtray.

I kept my feet on the floor and sat straight-backed. "I came because I haven't heard anything about Will's case being reopened."

He touched the cigar and it fell into the tray. "That's because it hasn't been."

I almost jumped out of the chair. "What do you mean?

You have the log. If you read it, it is hard evidence that Will wasn't suicidal! It could be used as a document in any court. If you look at the map, you can tell where he was digging."

"Well now, that just isn't the case. All the map shows is that he dug in several areas on Pine Island. There is nothing that showed where he was digging the week before his death. And the log? From what I read it sounded like a guy saying goodbye to the world. I think he even said something about never hunting again. Those are the words of a man who gave up. We called the county historic society and Will's chest was delivered the morning after his death. He must have made arrangements after he wrote in the log. So, you see, Ms. Murphy, he wasn't killed by a thief as you probably suspect. The poor man was despondent and ended his own life. He fulfilled a dream and felt worse. He was a process man. Life disappointed him. He had a bad role model as a father. His sister told me the sad family story."

I was stunned and although surprised by the information about the chest, was positive he was wrong. My fingers tightened into fists. "Will Rolins *was* murdered. Murdered!"

"My dear, I don't know how many times I have to say this. Will Rolins committed suicide. Have you found any concrete evidence showing he did *not* do it?"

"No! But, Sheriff, I do have more information concerning the night he was murdered. I have it first-hand that Rose Thompson and a man were seen outside Will's duplex on the night of his death."

"And who is the witness?"

"Taco, a waitress at Bert's."

The sheriff's facial muscles twitched. He took his hands off his desk and placed them on either side of his chair. "I see." He stretched his neck, making his wing nut ears twitch. "Well, we'll have to look into that allegation." He picked up a pen.

I had the urge to find a wrench. "I have other information about Rose." Looking him directly in the eyes, I spoke rapidly. I told him about my suspicions about Rose's position on abortion, how she had most likely overheard talk about finding an abortion clinic between Will and Taco, how I had followed her to a house and overheard talk about a bombing, and how I had made an anonymous phone call to the police. "You see, Sheriff, I don't think the motive for Will's murder was theft. I think it was a hate crime."

"You suspect Rolins was killed because he helped someone get an abortion?"

I nodded vigorously.

The sheriff lowered his head and wrote on a tablet. When he raised it again, he slowly put down his pen and intertwined his fingers. "Thank you for this information, Ms. Murphy. It will be looked into. But I do want to say again, that whoever told you the vandalism to your motel room meant you were being threatened did you a disservice. At the most, you were targeted for a sick prank, nothing else. Who was it that said this, by the way?"

"Rose Thompson, who I believe is either an Army of God terrorist herself or in some way assists the movement."

"That's a weighty allegation."

"I was also being followed," I added.

He leaned forward. "You know this for a fact?"

"Someone saw it happening."

"Who?"

"Jay Mann."

"I see. The sculptor. Matlacha is so full of artists, isn't it?" He didn't exactly sneer, but he sure as heck sniffed. Jerk.

"Can I assume that you've deduced that Rose was trying to throw you off the track?"

Like, duh!

He was holding back a smile. I wanted to punch him.

He continued. "That you might have been seen leaving the house that night after you followed her and The Army of God has you on some kind of hit list. Is that your conclusion?"

I frowned. "Well, that does sound a bit melodramatic."

"I'm glad you see that, Ms. Murphy. I understand you're also an artist?"

"Yes, so?"

"Artists are noted for having vivid imaginations, isn't that right, my dear?"

I closed my eyes and pressed my lips together, working hard at controlling my anger.

This was not the first time someone had used those words or that tone with me. When working for the private eye agency I'd been told by Hawk's partner that I didn't have the DNA or reasoning skills to even be a helpful administrative secretary. It took me a few months to get over that ego hit.

"It couldn't be that by this woman reinforcing the threat the night of the vandalism and suggesting that you leave Matlacha that perhaps she has come to like you and doesn't want to see you harmed?"

Well…

"Is there anything else, my dear?"

If he said "my dear" one more time I swore I was sure to level him.

"All I'm asking is that you investigate everything I've told you."

He assured me that all my allegations would be explored, but I could see he was thinking he had better things to do with his time.

I asked if he would let me know when Will's case was re-opened. He said he would personally make the call and inquired into whether I wanted a deputy to be assigned to protect me. Seething, I said it wouldn't be necessary. I had the impression he didn't think so either.

Lucky for him, he kept any further endearments to himself.

I hurried out of the office feeling less than happy with how the meeting went, but realizing the sheriff would have to investigate and when he did, the official search for Will's murderer would begin. Floridians were noted to be slow and this guy would probably come in last at an aardvark race.

Believing I would be leaving early the following week and feeling an urge to sketch another place Will and I had once enjoyed, I drove to the Cape Coral Yacht Club beach. I was soon sitting on the bench of a picnic table under a palm tree sketching my anger away.

A man walked by and craned his neck to see my sketch pad. I re-adjusted my shoulder to block his view and turned my tan cap around to the back. With slow movements I sketched the long fishing dock, the café, a trawler cruising on the river. Turning the page, I began to sketch again the faces of Rose, Bill, Lil, Taco, Jay, Sheriff Schilling, Luke, the Lakewoods, even Gator.

Children bobbed up and down in the water, taking in the sun. They laughed and flapped the surface as their mothers and fathers shaded by umbrellas watched from their beach towels.

Maybe one day. Having kids could expand my life. Grandma Murphy said I'd make a darn good mother.

A woman in a hot pink string bikini stood near the shelter house. A tween came out of the door. She had straggly sandy hair and the body of a gymnast.

I smiled at a child playing in front of her. The kid couldn't be two. His swim trunks bulged with diaper. The look on the child's face was thoughtful, contemplative. He seemed to be studying the sand under his feet. The breeze ruffled his baby-fine hair. I was struck by how totally self-contained the child appeared. I thought of Will. This is how he would have been at this age, self-contained and confident, able to strike out on his own; yet still in need of his mother to keep him safe. I stepped closer. Will's face appeared in my mind's eye; the smooth skin of his face smearing into an oval fading image, then snapping back into focus.

Sprinting forward, the young mother snatched up her child. "He's mine." Holding him close, she carried him back to her blanket and tented him with a towel.

Startled by the child's sudden disappearance and the mother's reaction, I continued down the shore, moving to an isolated area, dropping onto the sand. A boat motored by pulling a water skier. I felt fidgety. I stood, gathered my belongings and headed for my car. I stopped when I saw them—the burrowing owls. No bigger than six inches, they rested on a mound near the edge of a landscaped circle. A cross made out of thin strips of wood served as a perch. How amazingly peaceful and steadfast they were, even though traffic whizzed by and beachgoers stared. These owls lived underground. Whatever made them choose the earth for a home? It would be like me choosing not to know the facts after hearing about Will's death. Accepting blindly what I'd been told. That Will shot himself. Maybe it was a need to get away from the madness above ground. That I could understand. I stood ten feet from them. One scurried into the hole while the other stood its ground, keeping watch. I stepped closer. The bird flew to the cross, settled itself and continued to watch me. I wanted to draw it, but would the owl stay put? I took another cautious step.

A car back-fired. I turned. The owl shot away.

"You're not to bother them. They're endangered."

The sheriff. Swallowing the quick retort that came to my lips, I turned to him and made myself show him the teeth Grandma Murphy was so proud of. "Yes, I know, Sheriff. Aren't they something?"

His expression wasn't friendly. "Just remember to keep your distance. Getting too close makes them nervous."

The phrase gave me pause. Surely it wasn't a slip of the tongue. I hadn't made *him* nervous, had I?

"And don't get any notion that I'm following you."

That hadn't occurred to me until he mentioned it, but now…well…hmm…

"Ms. Murphy, when are you leaving?"

"If I didn't know better, I'd say, you're trying to get rid of me."

"My dear, I am really worried about your state of mind. You're speaking the words of a very paranoid person. We all just want the best for you."

Yeah, right.

I drew my sketch pad close to my chest. I was so glad I hadn't brought Gar to the beach. That would have clinched this guy's opinion of me. Not that I cared. It wasn't like he had any authority to commit me or anything. "You'll call me when you re-open Will's case?" I asked.

"Absolutely, my dear."

Making my voice sugary sweet, I said, "I'll be leaving soon. I do need to get away from all these reminders of Will." I sidled away and then turned. "By the way, Sheriff, were you the one who answered the call the night Will died?" I could check this out against the report Hawk had sent, but he didn't know that.

His frown contorted his face. "As a matter of fact, my dear, I was in Tampa that week. I was never in Will's apartment."

I found out later he hadn't lied. His name was nowhere on the report, but that didn't mean he hadn't been there.

18

A lemon beside an orange ceases being a lemon, and the orange an orange, and they become fruits.
~ Georges Braque

It had been three days since my living space had been vandalized. Three days since I'd seen Rose go into a house where I heard talk of violence and words of hate.

I now doubted the sheriff's honesty and began to have snippets of suspicions that he had something to do with Will's murder. What had Will written that Gator had told him? Every man is a con man. Apparently even the thick-skinned, dick-dominated, wing nut-eared lawman had this potential.

Go figure.

Hugging Gar, I took him to the table under the window. I sat him down gently and began to devise my next plan of action. I needed hard evidence against Rose. I knew that. Taco held that key. But could I trust the sheriff to question Taco? To get her to file a report? Could I trust him to investigate my allegations against Rose? Not likely. I would give him until Monday. If nothing was done I'd contact the police in the next county.

My thoughts went to Taco. What she had seen proved

nothing. Rose could have been visiting Gator and his partner. It was a duplex after all. I stood. I'd go find Gator. At least he could answer that question. Then I'd take another look at Will's apartment to see if I'd missed anything.

If Gator wasn't fishing on the bridge or in his office in front of the store, I'd go to the duplex. Hopefully, I'd find him there.

"Don't worry, Gar. I've got my phone," I said. "It's broad daylight. I'll be fine."

It was 2 p.m. The noise being made by the construction workers was deafening. Gator was not on the bridge or in his office. I headed for May Street. Several tourists swinging shopping bags passed me. A couple licking waffle cones nodded and smiled before the young woman climbed onto the seat of the super-sized rocking chair in front of a shop. Her mate took a picture. The flag in front of the post office hung limp. To all appearances it was a lazy, peaceful day on the island. No one, besides me, knew that a murderer and perhaps terrorists lurked in our midst.

Using my knuckle, I tapped three times on the duplex door. No answer. I tapped again and heard movement inside. An osprey flew overhead, his headless catch dangling from his talons. The door opened.

"Hey, Gator," I said.

He was bare-chested, wore his usual cut-offs and had on bunny slippers. He grinned broadly when he saw me. "Why look who's here. Come on in. We were just going to have an afternoon drink to start off the weekend festivities."

He led me to the small screened-in porch at the back where two women sat, chatting. "Les, you two have met. But Zen, how about you? You met?"

I shook her hand as we were introduced to each other.

She was at least ten years younger than Les. Probably twenty years younger than Gator. She carried an extra thirty pounds around her belly and on her thighs and butt. Her hair was black and cut close to her scalp. Her round, flawless complexion reminded me of the favorite baby doll I had had as a kid. I liked her instantly.

Les passed out beers and I took one as we chatted about the weather and how good the fishing was last night.

Zen took a long drink of her beer before speaking. "We hear you're asking a lot of questions about Will's death. You don't think he killed himself, do ya?"

I was astounded. So much for my purpose in Matlacha being a secret. "I, ah, knew him real well and even though he was on anti-depressants, he wasn't the type to kill himself—not that there is a type—but with a gun? Will? It's hard to believe."

Zen rubbed her chin. "Yeah. We don't think he did it either."

"So, you knew him?" I asked.

"We used to sit out back and chew the fat at the end of the day. That guy was in love—he wasn't ready to suck no pistol."

I closed my eyes and rubbed my forehead, regrouping. It felt good to have someone say this. I let out all the air I'd been holding since Zen spoke, opened my eyes and nodded at her. I mouthed the words "thank you" before taking the biggest swallow of beer I'd ever had. Coughing, beer sprayed from my mouth.

Zen and Gator laughed. Les was out of the room.

"Will said you weren't much of a drinker," Zen said. "Guess he knew what he was talkin` about."

I wiped my lips and asked the question I'd come to ask.

"Either of you happen to see Rose Thompson hanging around your duplex the night Will died?"

"You mean the waitress from Bert's?" Gator asked.

"Yeah."

Gator and Zen said no and Les yelled the same reply from the kitchen.

"Someone say she was here?" Gator asked.

"No," I said.

"Well, there you have it. We wouldn't know anyways. Me and Les was fishing."

"I told you that before," Les called out from the kitchen.

"Oh, yeah. I remember. Zen, don't suppose you saw anything?"

"I wasn't anywhere near here. Sorry."

I set down my unfinished beer, wishing I could trust these people so I could unload further, but decided that was unwise.

Zen's eyes twinkled. "You know, I tried college once. It was a bust. My roommates spent all day, every day, playing poker. I was flabbergasted. I was shocked. I went broke."

Gator threw back his head and roared. Me and Les laughed, but not so much.

I had the feeling that Zen told the joke to lighten my load. And I appreciated that. I winked at Zen, stood, thanked them and said my farewells. I just had time to inspect Will's apartment again before getting ready to go to the gallery. I went outside, closed the door, took the key from my jean's pocket and attempted to insert it in the lock. But it didn't fit. I frowned and tried again. Les must have heard me muttering, because through the opened window of their duplex she said, "They gutted the apartment yesterday and changed the locks, hon. The owner said he wanted to get rid of, well, you know."

I gave Les a quick wave and tossed the useless key in the plastic bucket near a bush. I didn't blame the owner. I'd have it gutted it too—as fast as possible.

Frowning, I bent toward the bucket which was obviously also used as an ashtray. A cigar was buried in the sand. Only the tip showed. I caught my lip between my upper teeth. Knowing something about evidence, fingerprints and the like, I knew I shouldn't touch it. Using my smartphone, I first took several pictures of it where it was.

Next, I picked up a scrap of cardboard from a discarded cereal box that lay nearby and used it as a scoop. Gingerly I lifted a generous amount of the dirt, making sure the cardboard didn't touch the cigar. I set it on the ground, went to the other door and knocked. Les was happy to give me a plastic bag. I bagged the cigar. Perhaps fingerprints or teeth marks would prove who had left it. I already knew who smoked this brand— the sheriff. It was too late to get it to the Collier County police station. I was to be at Luke's gallery by five. It was 4:45. I didn't want to miss even a minute of the first night where one of my paintings hung in the gallery.

I was excited about the possibility of having hard evidence to prove that the sheriff was at Will's apartment, and I was nervous about the show.

I tripped twice and almost tumbled once as I hurried back to my efficiency.

Well, whatever.

19

A primitive artist is an amateur whose work sells.
~ *Grandma Moses*

I dressed quickly in the pale lavender sundress I'd found at Kiwanis and black flip flops I bought at Today's Hope Thrift Store before walking slowly to the gallery. I was pleased and surprised to see that the parking spaces were taken, both on the street and behind the gallery.

Soft Jamaican music played. Multi-colored Christmas lights were draped across the ceiling. A Bird of Paradise flower arrangement adorned a tie-dyed cloth. A heaping bowl of strawberries and a dish of melted chocolate sauce over a warming candle made my mouth water. Wine bottles, several types of soda and stemmed glasses lined the far end.

Dressed in a white silk shirt and dark chinos, Luke was behind the table chatting and laughing with an elderly couple. So handsome. So self-assured. I couldn't have felt more nervous. When he saw me enter, he motioned for me to join them. Several other customers in Florida evening attire were walking around the rooms, glasses in hand, admiring the artwork.

"You look lovely." Luke took my arm and introduced me

to the couple who chatted for several minutes then drifted away.

He passed me a glass of wine. After that beer I'd chugged, I only pretended to take a sip. I peered over Luke's shoulder to see why people were smiling toward the two carved, yellow-crowned herons flanking the entrance. At first I thought they were admiring the black and white faces and coal and milky wings of the whimsical birds, but I soon saw their attention was on the stunning Esther Lakewood. She was dressed in an ankle-length, screen-print, crinkly cotton sundress and was posing like a model. Her eyes darted about the room, landing on Luke. I sneaked a look toward him to see if he had noticed. He hadn't. His head was turned as he shook hands with a patron. I continued to watch Esther, who had to know she was attracting attention.

Luke stepped close. "Here's to a successful night, my lovely one," he said.

My cheeks reddened. We were surrounded by customers and they had to have heard the endearment. Luke, oblivious to my discomfort, placed his hand protectively on the small of my back and bragged about my work. Flushed and embarrassed, I stumbled out answers to questions about subject matter and technique and assured many I would have business cards made, although I knew I never would. After they moved on, I squeezed Luke's arm. "This is all a bit intimidating."

"It always is at first. Relax. Your work deserves all the praise it gets."

"I bet you say that to everyone who displays in your gallery."

"You bet I do," he said, chuckling.

The room buzzed with low conversation. Luke exuded charm and attentiveness. Continually, he filled glasses and greeted patrons, directing the attention to my painting. Esther was no longer in sight. Looking for another familiar face, I did a half-turn and saw Jay. He was gazing at Taco who had just walked into the room looking sexy as ever in a flowered sleeveless mini-dress. I wasn't jealous. Not at all.

"Excuse me," Luke said softly into my ear and walked away.

I kept my attention on Jay and Taco. A woman with white hair stopped in front of me and began to talk. But my attention was on the voluptuous Taco and handsome Jay Mann who were chatting in an earnest manner. Taco laughed, flipped her head and quickly looked toward Rose who had just entered the gallery. Across the room, Luke headed toward me, but I saw him take in Jay and Taco, and do an about-face. I dragged my attention away when I heard the older woman say that she had bought my painting. The blood left my face. At the price Luke had put on it? Really?

I gave the woman my full attention. "Why, thank you," I said, "I'm so glad you like it."

The woman said she particularly liked the eyes. In fact, she felt almost as if they followed her around the room. She gushed that she just had to own the painting.

I glanced up. In the mystical glow caused by the string of colorful Christmas lights the eyes did seem to be alive. I put my hand over my heart. The woman was right. They appeared to blink and take in the room. I shook my head. How ridiculous. It was a trick of twinkling lights that caused the life-like quality, nothing else. Yet, I too, couldn't take my gaze away. This woman must have as much superstitious Irish blood as I did. Absently, I said to her, "You know, if you paint something that has died, it's a way to bring it life again."

She took my free hand. "Why what a fascinating notion. You artists are so divinely creative."

Still mesmerized by the eyes, I jumped when Jay nudged my shoulder. His white, silk shirt made his tan appear darker. His eyes sparkled. I watched Taco head in the direction of the live music on the back patio followed by Rose. I took a sip of wine and introduced Jay to the customer.

"Jay's a talented sculptor," I said, feeling the warmth radiating from his arm against my shoulder before I leaned away.

The woman's grin was broad. "Do you have anything

here?"

"He doesn't show his work," I answered while Jay averted his eyes.

"Ah, hah, well, young man, if you ever decide to sell anything, let me know, and I'll take a look," she said, setting down her glass. "Well, I must be running along. Thank you, my dear, for painting such a divine picture." Her heels clicked the tile floor.

"Was she for real?" Jay asked.

I grinned. "Oh, yes. She bought my painting."

Luke breezed past and whispered in my ear, "I just heard you made us a nice little profit tonight. What did I tell you?" He moved on.

Jay and I turned as Rose's Bill walked in the door. He was clean-shaven and wearing a black cotton shirt, dress pants and leather sandals. Smiling broadly at me, he drifted by on the arm of a much younger woman in a pastel ankle-length dress. Intrigued, I watched them as they nodded at patrons, drank wine and smiled.

They went through the door to the patio as Rose stepped back in and came toward Jay and me. Jay, sniffing, walked away.

Rose glared at his retreating back. "Is *he* bothering you?"

"No, we were just chatting. Did you see Bill?"

Rose laughed. "Isn't he something?"

"Yeah, like a *totally*, I mean *totally* different man."

Which I supposed shouldn't surprise me that much, as he was most likely an accomplice with Rose in her terrorist activity. Anyway, that's how my mind was weaving.

Rose was dressed in a burgundy, polyester pantsuit lined in sequins. She had a white gold ring on every finger. "Taco's really enjoying the show. She's like a child. She's absolutely bonkers over those Disney plastic figures cemented around the garden. Under those colored lights she looks like Snow White herself. I had to leave. She's chatting with that dreadful Lakewood woman. I really don't see why that girl wants to associate with her. Hey, listen, do you want to join me for church on Sunday?"

I gave Rose a half-smile. "I'm not really a church-goer, but thanks for asking."

"God is a comfort," Rose said. "You really should join me. It would do you good."

I took another sip of wine as a male patron stopped in front of me and Rose slipped away.

Throughout the night, people strolled steadily in and out of the gallery. There was much talk about color palettes and the beauty of the night.

Not long after, Taco left alone, as did Rose. Soon the gallery was almost empty. The night had been a success. Four paintings had been sold. It was time to leave. Jay asked if he could walk me home. I agreed. As Jay and I strolled out of the gallery, Luke came to the doorway and congratulated me again. I said thanks and took Jay's arm.

The wind had picked up from the Gulf. The Fiddle Crabs Band was performing in front of the Olde` Fish House Marina not far from the street. The parking lot was filled with people in folding chairs. The food counter was open. I waved at Zen, who worked behind the counter and who'd spotted me and Jay.

"Want to set out back for a while?" Jay asked over the din of the music. "It's quieter there."

I said I would and went for drinks while Jay found us a picnic table near the water.

Zen accepted my order as she opened the refrigerator. "How'd it go tonight?"

"Pretty good. Someone bought my painting," I said, "but I'm glad it's over."

Zen laughed. "You're not the first artist to say that," she said. "It's one thing to create, another to sell. Here, they're on me. Got to support our local artists."

A man came up beside me to place his order. I thanked Zen and moved away.

The Fiddle Crabs had everyone smiling and clapping. I scanned the crowd, but saw no other familiar faces as I weaved through several people until I found Jay. He was sitting in front of a shrimp boat talking to a man at the next table. When I set the beer and soda in front of us, Jay turned to me and smiled.

I sat and raising our glasses we saluted each other. Jay turned his attention to the music. His eyes half closed as he listened. I thought about the exchange I'd observed at the show between him and Taco. Were they going to become an item? As if I cared. Unconsciously, I tapped a tune on the tabletop. It had surprised me to see Rose and Bill at the show. Why weren't they under arrest? Well, at least Rose.

My attention slid from the coconut fish I'd been absently looking at, but not seeing, to Jay's serious hazel eyes, now gazing at me. "What?" I said.

"Just worried about you."

I tipped my head to the right. "I'm a big girl. I can take care of myself. Besides, I'm leaving in a couple of days. I was just hanging around for the show." I saw Taco join a small group near the store entrance. "So, you're attracted to Taco, huh?"

I had to repeat the question because it appeared the words swept out to sea before Jay could catch them.

But when he raised his head, the look in his eyes was mischievous. "Taco? Sure. Who wouldn't be? She's a looker."

"And is it mutual?"

His eyes twinkled. "Is what mutual?"

"The attraction?"

He set down his bottle. "Taco attracted to me? Not yet, but things can change. I'm not one to give up on the first, second, or even third try." He grinned at me over the top of his bottle, appeared to be about to say something, but apparently changed his mind. He chugged his beer.

The music increased in tempo. The audience began to clap, stomp and sing along with the band.

I attempted to continue questioning Jay about Taco, but Jay's confession seemed to have made him lose interest in the subject.

The wind whistled down Matlacha Pass, stinging my face, but I didn't mind. I could think about the wind and the sting for a moment, instead of hoping that Rose and her cohorts would soon be behind bars and that Rose would admit to killing Will.

"By the way, congratulations. You're on your way," Jay said.

"Thanks, but on my way—where? I just sold one painting." But I knew as well as he, that doing so had boosted my self-confidence.

He looked at the canal and then back at me. "You have the right attitude about your work."

"I do?"

"Look at you. You're nonchalant, for Christ's sake. Aren't you thrilled? Don't you want to jump up and down?"

Oh my! To my embarrassment, I smiled a silly kid grin. Of course I was thrilled. More than thrilled. "Well, I suppose I should be."

"That's what I mean. You're one tough woman. You seemed so cool at the show."

If he only knew how anxious I was. I cleared my throat. "Well, I'm a good actress. The fact is I felt more nervous than a girl in her first strapless prom dress.

He gave me a quizzical look. "You didn't show it."

"I'm pretty good at hiding my feelings. Hey, why isn't your work in a gallery? Surely, you don't need Luke's help. There are plenty of other galleries in the area."

"I don't know how I would take the critical response or the thought that my work might not be appreciated."

Oh, yeah. This I get. Big time.

"Really?" But I totally understood. Grandma Murphy always said, fear of failure was a powerful, manipulating force, but, then, so was fear of success.

"Sure. It's easier to keep creating and ignoring the world than to face the rejections; at least then you can hang onto your fantasy that you might be good. When I was little, my mother used to be my worst critic. She didn't think anything I did was done right. I guess I haven't gotten over that."

"Parents…ah, parents…But can't you be good even though the particular work in the gallery doesn't appeal to the people who come in to view it?"

"Well, of course, but I need to feel like people will want to buy my work, so taking the risk that they might not…Well, I'm not sure how my ego would take the rejection. We have to know who we are. Although, I must admit, I guess I'd take the risk. If Abbot or another gallery offered to show some of my work, I'd go for it."

"So, why don't you propose the idea?"

"Pride. I'd like to be asked or someone else to suggest it."

Exactly what had happened to me. I wondered if Jay knew that.

I jumped at the sound of sirens. Our eyes locked. With raised eyebrows, we pushed ourselves off the wooden bench and without a word hurried in the direction of the bridge and the dreadful flashing lights and the already milling crowd.

Three cop cars and a pick-up were parked in front of Rose's cracker box rental house. The door was wide open. Rose and Bill were led out in handcuffs.

My heart pounded. I bit my lip. Finally. Results. Hallelujah.

Moments later the white and green cop car whizzed past us, sirens blaring. Jay took my arm and we followed the murmuring crowd to Bert's. The bar whirled with conjecture and raised voices: They're bank robbers. No, they're the ones who let all the air out of the tires on Velma Street last spring. No, I heard Bill offed his wife and Rose was the accomplice. Nah, they set fire to the Post Office. It's a federal offense.

I kept what I knew to myself. It wouldn't be long until the real story would come out in the papers and on the news. Who Rose and Bill were, was even worse than anyone could imagine—activists who set bombs to go off, killing innocent people.

Later in my room, kept awake by my thoughts, I tossed and turned as sweat beads formed on my head. Finally, I sat up and giving up on any hopes for sleep, I threw off the crumpled sheet and went to the window that I'd left open an inch.

A breeze wafted into the room. Waves rumbled against

pilings. I turned and began to pace. Sitting, I sketched, dropping the drawings one by one onto the floor, then stood up and continued to walk from one end of the room to the other. Again, I sat and drew.

At 5 a.m. I was still awake and the floor near my feet was cluttered. Exhausted, I pushed the sketches around with my big toe, my eyes locking onto one image—Taco's. I don't believe it. Oh my God! Setting down my tablet and drawing pencil, pulling Gar to me, a grim expression spread across my face as the light bulb in my head burned bright.

Why hadn't I seen the resemblance before?

Okay, don't jump to conclusions. First, double check to make sure the sheriff and Taco really are father and daughter, then call the police in the next county. So what if they are? Why would that be important? But why had neither of them told me they were related? What were they hiding?

Something definitely was not right in River City, not at all.

I needed to get back into the sheriff's office. Like yesterday.

20

I think that if you shake the tree, you ought to be around when the fruit falls to pick it up.

~ Mary Cassatt

The bench outside the sheriff's office was angled forward, cutting in just below my shoulder blade. Was it designed to make visitors uncomfortable? If so, it was well made. I leaned forward, half-listening to a different dispatcher at the desk talking on the phone. She was a sharp-boned woman with thick dishwater-blonde hair. She reminded me of a certain weather caster on one of the local channels in Boston. In fact, the woman could be the weather caster's sister. The dispatcher wore earphones that wrapped her head in a thin line of black plastic, making her look like she had on an old-fashioned headband. The speaking mechanism partially hid her lined-with-wrinkles lips.

I wondered if the woman knew that the device messed up her hair. She didn't seem like the type who would take kindly to such abuse. When the call ended she glanced my way. Her grim look said "Are you still here?" but she kept the question to herself. In my mind, I gave her the finger.

Sorry Grandma.

"I'm not sure when the sheriff will return. I told you that, right?"

I gave her a broad, innocent smile, one meant to disarm. "I have all the time in the world." I ducked my head and picked up a magazine.

My hopes were that if I hung around long enough either the sheriff would return and I'd follow him into his office, or if not that, I'd find a way to sneak in when the weather woman's sister wasn't looking. I know. I know. I couldn't be arrested for trespass. But I only wanted a quick photo. I could get that by not stepping into the room.

A cop came out of the secure door, dropped a sheet of paper on the dispatcher's desk and without glancing at me, left the building.

I pretended I was reading. Patience was not one of my virtues, especially when I was nervous. It was 11 a.m. An hour before the average person took a lunch break. Surely this woman, who definitely tipped toward the average scale, didn't bring her lunch. I flipped a page. The phone buzzed again. As the woman talked she gazed over her glasses at me. I could tell my presence irritated her. To defuse the negativity I smiled again, imagining a sudden splash of light shot from one of my front teeth. One of the woman's eyelids lowered. Her lips did a tightening and untightening thing. I invisibly shrugged and half-turned.

A couple came in the door, hurried to the dispatcher, mumbled inaudible words, then left again.

I buried my face in the magazine. I was a betting woman. Oh, I didn't go to casinos and gamble or play poker like some of my friends and family, but I bet on stuff, usually against myself, but not always. Like who was going to become the next American Idol. Or, who would win the Super Bowl. Of course, the fact I thought it was basketball season during football season had certainly caused much laughter. Oh, well. Laughter was good for you. Even if it's you someone was laughing at. Once I won a free dinner cooked every week for a month from Hawk. Another time I'd had to do his laundry for two weeks. Things like that. Right now I bet a quarter that the woman had her lunch at that café and that I could get my photos without being seen.

I felt like Dorothy waiting to see the wizard, anguished, child-like, and anxious. My leg bounced up and down. Sighing I dropped the magazine, eyeing the wall clock. If my hunch was right I'd be calling the Collier County police force real soon.

Thank you that she leaves soon. Thank you that she leaves soon, I repeated to myself.

"So, how are the lunch specials at the café next door?" I asked, hoping my mention of the place maybe, just maybe, would make the woman's stomach remember it was hungry. "They sure make a good latte`."

She eyed me blankly.

I hated it when government workers acted as if they were serious about their jobs. Who did she think she was trying to kid?

"I eat at one sharp," she finally said. It was 12:50.

I pulled my drawing pad out of my carry bag and began to sketch. The dispatcher was hidden now behind a computer screen. I wiggled my toes as I drew to the soft, steady clicking of the keyboard.

At five minutes to one the clicking stopped. "I'm going to lunch now," the woman announced in the same tone an attendant used at an airport for the last call to board.

I pretended I was too absorbed in my drawing to hear. I did not stop my hand movement.

Thank you that I got that secure door open. Thank you that I got into the sheriff's office. Thank you that I'm not caught.

The woman cleared her throat and repeated her announcement. I ignored her.

Silence fell over the room. I could feel the woman's frustration. See, I'm too busy. I'm harmless, I attempted to transmit telepathically.

I began to shade the neck of the woman's likeness as I continued to do my intentions.

"So, you're an artist?" the dispatcher asked.

I slowly raised my head and shared once again my sparkling smile. "Oh, yes," I said in my most naive, distracted voice, ducking my head and continuing to work.

"Okay, then. I don't want to interrupt you. I have a niece who writes and getting her attention when she's writing is like landing a tarpon from a kayak, nearly impossible, least that's what my sweetie says. So, hon, I'll be back in half an hour. Most likely the sheriff will return while I'm gone. Officer Perry will be returning from lunch soon. You be good now."

Her rubber heels tapped the terrazzo floor as she made it for the exit.

She hesitated and patted her hair back into place. I assumed she was very aware of the hair messing issue. Salary had triumphed over fashion.

A cop, most likely Perry, hurried in through the entrance of the building. Ignoring me, he pushed numbers on the security box, opened the door wide and disappeared. I jumped and hearing him moving fast down the corridor, slid my toe between the door jamb and the door. I waited. A door opened and shut. I was in luck. I waited one more minute and then opened the door and stepped through. If the Universe was with me on this, the sheriff had not locked his office. Hurrying down the corridor, I stopped short. I put my hand on the knob. It turned. "Thank you," I mouthed.

Throwing common sense out the open window, I hastened in, leaving the door ajar. I went behind the desk chair and snapped photos with my smartphone from several angles. Then on a hunch I sat in the sheriff's chair and began opening drawers. The usual paperwork. A bottle of whiskey. A drawer full of very, very old gold coins. Gold coins? Swallowing, and glancing over my shoulder, I plucked one coin out of the drawer and dropped it into my pocket. Placing the other coins into a triangle, I hoped the sheriff had a short memory on how many he had. In less than three minutes, I was in and out. I shut the secured door with a soft click, looked around (the dispatcher's chair was empty) and ran out the front door, breathless. I was behind my steering wheel before the weather woman's sister had her chicken salad.

Safe in my car I tilted my head back. What did all this mean? Why did the sheriff have the coins? Was he a mere collector? Did they belong to another case? Or were they from Will's find? I put my bet on the latter speculation. If it could be proved that they were from the same chest that ended up at the historic society, then couldn't that be used as evidence against the sheriff? Could the sheriff have decided that it was too dangerous for him to keep the chest after killing Will? Could he have had it delivered that night? Yes and yes.

I studied the photos. There was no doubt this was father and daughter. But what did the fact the sheriff was Taco's dad have to do with anything? Taco had said she hadn't spoken to her dad in years after he helped put her brother in jail. So she wasn't necessarily involved. The sheriff had been trying to send me packing since I'd arrived in Matlacha. A sheriff's salary couldn't be much. The sucker was probably as greedy as Midas.

Using my phone GPS I followed the directions to the historic society's office. Surely they could tell me if the coin matched those that were found in the chest the sheriff said Will donated to them. Like through DNA or something.

The man I spoke to was aware of the Rolins donation. After hearing of Will's suicide, he said they had contacted his next of kin—his sister. She had told them she wanted nothing to do with the treasure. As far as she was concerned, it belonged to the State of Florida.

Millie generous? There must have been a nun listening to the phone call. A nun Millie would try to impress with an act of goodness.

"Where did you get this?" the man at the office asked.

For me to know and you to find out.

"I'll tell you that later," I said. "I just want to know if these are from the same chest that Will Rolins sent you."

"We'll have to do some tests, but they sure look similar. It's most likely the same year. But that proves nothing. I'll have to get back to you."

"How long will it take?"

"If the lab tech isn't swamped, we should know by five tonight. If she is, it could be as late as the end of next week."

I provided my phone number and walked to my car, focusing on what my next move should be. Wasn't I the one who was going to be out of here right after the show? I glanced at the clock. I would just make my luncheon engagement—one I didn't plan to miss. Jay Mann had raised my curiosity with a promise of a surprise. I liked surprises, as long as they didn't include a gun pointing at my heart.

I made a stop at a veggie stand, and then continued west.

When I strolled in Jay's door he was barefoot, wore a frayed pair of cut-off jeans, and a gray T-shirt that fit tight across his chest. Scanning the room for the dogs, I stepped out of my flip flops.

"About time," he said.

I looked right to left. "I brought the salad."

"Excellent. Oh, I put the dogs in the bedroom. I seem to remember they made you nervous."

I released the breath I'd been holding in. "How's your newest project coming along?" I put fresh lettuce, endive, peppers, and cherry tomatoes in the fridge, laying the pine nuts on the counter. I assumed he had dressing.

"I'm trying something new—working kind of Giacometti small—if you know what I mean."

"No, can't say that I do."

Jay picked up one of his statues, a man holding a fishing pole or spear. "Albert Giacometti was one of the finest sculptors in the world. He had a period of time when he became obsessed with perfecting pieces. As he worked on them, they kept getting smaller and smaller until they were tiny as pin heads."

"Whoa!"

"Yeah, well, I got his bug and, well…I'm kind of doing

that myself right now."

"Can I see one of the miniatures?"

"Nah. Not for showing just yet. What about you?" He set down the statue, went to the sink and began cleaning shrimp. The double sliding glass door leading to the sea was open. The fan overhead whirled. I was going to miss this.

"I fluctuate between painting birds with Will's eyes, to sketching faces." Absently, I picked up the romaine, knowing that I was actually really, really stuck on getting Will's killer arrested. Of course, maybe they already were. Rose and Bill were in jail: But the sheriff, the coins, and the secrecy around Taco as possibly his daughter—that was more than bothersome.

The wind grabbed the plate of shrimp shells and sent them flying. The metal plate crashed onto the floor. The Rottweilers whined. Jay bent to clean up the mess. This reminded me of a time I'd knocked a plate of crab on the floor and Will had told me how his mother would have had a fit if he'd done that, which led me to ask my next question. "Since your never became friends, I'm sure Will never talked about his parents?"

"Oddly enough he did. In fact, it was at our second meeting. I got a phone call from my dad who is still a flaming hippie and when I told him that, he brought up his parents. He said they were incredibly straight—not a bohemian ounce of blood in them. We laughed about the differences."

"I can hear Will saying that." Rinsing, and then separating the lettuce, I asked, "Did he mention his father committed suicide?"

"No, he didn't. You know, you'll probably never find out the real reason he did what he did, but I understand your need to."

I let that pass. It didn't seem like the right time to be honest with Jay about my true reason for still being in Matlacha. I would have to come clean, eventually, but I wasn't ready yet.

We carried the meal to his back dock. Music filtered across the water from Bert's. Water lapped against his boat. A cormorant sat on the nearest piling, wings wide as he dried them. We chatted about art as we watched pelicans plunge dive and feed.

As two dolphin rose from the water, the dogs began to bark. The door to the bedroom rattled.

Jay stood. "There must be someone at the gate. Be right back."

Carrying our plates I went into the studio and inspected a medium-sized statue of a woman sitting on a table at the far end of the room. It was an intriguing, misshapen figure. Her breasts were small. Her head was the shape of a pear and her torso was incredibly thin and elongated. I wondered if this was one of the pieces that would be miniaturized.

"My view is worth seeing." Jay re-entered the room with Esther Lakewood at his side. "You remember Jessie Murphy?"

Esther's expression became a knotty pine board. "Why, absolutely, the painter from Boston whose, ah, boyfriend committed suicide after she deserted him. How charming that you're here."

My gaze traveled from Esther who was gazing hungrily at Jay, to Jay, who erased a look of shock and displeasure from his face so fast that I almost missed it. But, not quite.

"Yes. What a surprise, Mrs. L."

"Oh, do, please call me Esther." Her glance held dismissal. "I just came from that quaint little bar." She eyed Jay as if he were a piece of chocolate cake drizzled with hot chocolate sauce. "I must see this young man's works of art. I understand they're more than delightful." She raked his body for every possible weed she could find. Finding none, she beamed like a lightning bug in heat.

"Ah, but I hardly ever show them." He leaned back against the table, crossing his arms over his broad chest, one foot over the other.

"Nonsense. I have an instinct for quality. I won't budge an inch out of this charming, bohemian home until you share some of your pieces," she purred.

Not impressed with the woman's false sense of

entitlement, I turned my back. Jay had seemed to be weighing the situation, and I hoped, was attempting to figure out how tactfully to get rid of the evil woman he had just invited into his home and studio. However, apparently Esther's fake flattery and commanding presence had its effect. He hurried to a door and disappeared. Esther strolled to the statue I had been admiring.

"I knew it," she said in triumph. "He has talent."

I had to work hard at not rolling my eyes. Real hard. I returned to the sink and turned on the faucet.

"Are you sleeping with him?"

Blood rushed from my face. I dropped the silverware.

Esther exploded in a high-pitched laugh. "Not very subtle of me, right? So sorry, but I like to know right away who my competition is. I've never been good at being devious."

Looking at the profile of the gorgeous, middle-aged witch in the white pants and handprint blouse, I refused to respond. I was in mourning. What was she thinking?

"It doesn't matter, of course. Money and my looks always win out," Esther said.

"I bet," I mumbled. Well, I'm sorry, Grandma, but she did ask for it.

Esther pivoted toward me. A smile played on her lips. "There are certain things, my dear, that are hard to compete with."

This time I wasn't able to swallow my disdain. "Like me, for instance?"

Jay hurried back into the room. "I have a couple of pieces you can see in here."

"Ah. Perfect." In a flourish, Esther took his elbow. "Do show them to me." She flipped her thick hair off her shoulder as they disappeared into the room.

I glowered at the dishes and walked outside and went to the end of the dock. A sturdy, white houseboat motored into the channel. The vessel ran up the pass a little farther, and then anchored not far from shore. The boat was showing her age, but still was a beauty, just like Esther Lakewood, who had apparently discovered all sorts of riches in that room. Esther giggled. Jay really!

Brilliant." Esther stepped into the fan-cooled room."Set a price."

Curious, I came back into the house.

Without hesitation, Jay named an exorbitant amount that made my head spin.

"Done."

Jay didn't flinch. He bowed his head slightly and said, "I'll deliver it tomorrow." He placed his hand over his heart like some guru, making me want to gag.

"Absolutely perfection, dar…ling. You have my card." In triumph, Esther turned to me and gave me a perfunctory nod. "Must run." And she flew out the door on her broom.

Jay grinned sheepishly and sat. I could see his muscles move under the cotton as he leaned forward.

"Well, that was a surprise," he said. "I just sold my first piece. Can you believe it?"

"Why does that surprise you? You believe they're good. You said so yourself. But selling to that woman? Get out!"

"Yeah, well, the situation was a bit unorthodox, but is there something wrong with her money?"

"No, but it would make me ill imagining my art in her home. She asked if I slept with you." Jay had just dropped two notches on my respect gauge.

"You don't think it's my art she admires, do you?"

He was kidding, right? "Do you?"

I started when my phone exploded with monkey laughter. It was the man about the coin. As I talked, I walked out of earshot. The coin was the same year, but it would take more tests to prove anything else. It would have to be sent to a different lab, one in Georgia. He asked again where I got it. I assured him I would enlighten him soon and ended the call. Now what?

I strolled over to the table where I'd seen Jay's coins, but they were gone. I asked him where they were. He said he was having them made into necklaces. I wondered.

Just when you thought you had a person figured out, a spit ball was thrown.

Jay came and stood beside me. "Shall we go?"

"Go where?"

"The surprise. Remember?"

After the Esther incident, I wasn't sure I wanted to spend any more time with Jay. I put my cap on my head. "Oh, yeah. Well, perhaps another time. I've got something important to do."

"Ah, come on. Can't it wait for an hour? I'll have you back by then."

I made myself not sniff. "Where is this surprise?"

"Just west of St. James City. We'll take my boat. I promise to make it quick."

A boat ride? I hadn't been on the water since my brief kayak trip. Of course I'd reconsider. Another hour wouldn't matter. The sheriff didn't suspect me of anything other than being a ditsy, no-brain-in-her-head artist. He wasn't going anywhere. I smiled and told Jay I would go.

Not long after, shooting between red and green markers, using Jay's binoculars, I inspected a mangrove rookery where a dozen or so pelicans were settled. But I wasn't reflecting on the nesting birds. I was deliberating on what I should do about the sheriff. I had proof that he was in possession of a coin, that was all. Even if it was from Will's treasure, did that prove he had murdered Will? No. Perhaps if I confronted him—took him by surprise—I could make him slip up. But that was dangerous. There had to be something wiser to do. But I was too young to be wise—way too young. In fact, even when I was old, I doubted I would be wise.

"That's St. James City," Jay yelled over the roar of the engine.

"Lots of boats out today," I called back as the boat rocked in wakes caused by bigger vessels passing on either side of us.

"Busy? You bet. It's the weekend. All the boaters are out playing with their toys. Look at all the jet skis. Looks like a motorway playground. That Grady White is going way too fast. Look at the wake she's making. Hold on."

Jay shot a look at me. I gave him a weak smile and held tight until the confused waters smoothed out again. I'd never been seasick, but there was always a first time.

"Nothing makes me madder than inconsiderate captains. They're a menace to us all."

"Think you've settled here for good?" I asked as we approached a smaller island.

"Ah, never sure of that. What about you, are you settled up north?"

"I, uh… don't know…"

"Matlacha seems a natural for you. When do you head back?"

"Soon. I have a job waiting for me."

"We're not so different, you and I. Both of us are artists trying to figure out how to live the life." He gave me a solemn but warm grin. "Okay, this is it. Could you hop onto the dock? I'll toss you a line."

"Absolutely no gators here, right?

"It's Florida. Just stay close."

After getting off, he secured another line then took my elbow. "The house is over this way. Wait until you see it. It's a beauty. My investor said he and his partner got a steal. Ah, here we are the four-million-dollar island wonder."

"Oh!"

The windows of the three-story, stilt house sparkled. I wondered who kept them so clean.

"It's the only house on the island. Come on, you've got to see the inside."

We climbed the stairs and walked around the deck. Below us, a small soaking pool was surrounded by thick mangrove. The island appeared to be about the size of two or three house lots. Foliage covered most of it. A narrow path wound from the boat dock to the far end where I could see a small clearing. One side of the island was lined by a narrow shore, the other areas were covered by greenery to the water's edge. I had to admit, I could imagine putting a kayak out from here and I definitely could see myself painting on this deck. "My, my!" I said with rounded eyes.

"You haven't seen anything yet." Jay unlocked the door and held it open, motioning for me to enter.

The living room had thirty-foot ceilings, a white mantled fireplace, pine floors and was fitted with brown overstuffed, Tommy Bahama furniture. The kitchen had a beaded ceiling, white cabinets, a large marble countered center island and stainless steel Bosch appliances. A table in an adjoining den had a chess set positioned in the center.

Whew! So cool. "Ah, so this is how the other half lives," I mumbled. "I should have brought Gar. He would have loved this."

Jay, who had climbed another flight of stairs, stuck his head over the railing and grinned. "Check out the view from up here."

I smiled and climbed the staircase. "All you can see is water and boats. Give me a break!"

"That's Sanibel in the distance." He turned and motioned with a sweep of his arm. "This is the bedroom."

The room was almost filled with a net draped four-poster white bed.

"Nice."

"The tour's not over yet. Follow me." He stepped out the door.

I followed him around a four-foot deck. A spiral staircase led up to a third-floor observation area. An even better place to paint. "You're kidding me!" I exclaimed. "Look at the view from up here! It's incredible."

"Check out the lagoon, there must be a dozen dolphins."

"I'd be happy on this island in a tent."

"Even without a tent," he said.

I frowned at him. "So, exactly why did you bring me here?"

"The owners are looking for someone to help take care of this place. This is only one of their properties. You came to mind. Make a great painter's paradise, don't you think?"

My eyes widened. "What?"

"All they want is for someone to watch over the house, make sure the generator is working, that no one's broken in—that kind of thing. For that, you get a free place to stay, an island to yourself and a view that would inspire Picasso. You'd be house sitting."

I was glad he hadn't said, "And wash the windows." When I got through washing a window, shine is not what it did.

"Wow!" I circled the room, taking it all in, considering.

"An offer worth pondering, wouldn't you say?" His eyes were inviting. His smile was teasingly tempting me.

"Why don't *you* take the owner up on it?"

"I've already got a million-dollar view."

I placed my hands on the railing, amazed at the proposal. Was this something I could do? Had the Universe just offered me a gift I couldn't refuse?

Jay smiled at me. "I guess I should be honest. I wasn't the first one to have the idea. Before Will and I had our, ah, misunderstanding, I brought him here. He's the one who suggested it was perfect for you."

I made a clicking sound, blinked back tears, and let the cool breeze cool my neck. I could imagine Will wanting this for me. How many times had he encouraged me to take my painting seriously? I tapped the railing and gazed out to sea. If I lived here, I'd only need enough money to buy food and pay for the utilities. Did I have enough saved to make it a year without a part-time job? Could I live on an island alone? Wouldn't I be too lonely? A pelican swooped low across a palm tree and landed on a branch. With the slow motion of a turtle, its head turned and it gazed at me. Of course I thought of Will.

My head felt like it would explode. Tears moistened my eyes. Get control of yourself. You have work to do.

Excusing myself, blinking rapidly, I walked inside. Pulling my phone from my pocket, I phoned the sheriff. "Hello. This is Jessie Murphy."

"Why, Miss Murphy. Just the woman I'd like to talk to. I'm tied up until after six, but could you meet me tonight at seven at my office?"

Cautiously agreeing, I slid the phone into my pocket. Great. Seven tonight when no one else was around. Another murder suspect wanting to meet me in isolation.

Jay walked to my side. "Everything okay?"

"Oh, sure. Shall we head back?" I knew I needed help this time, someone who wouldn't let me get injured or maimed too badly. Maybe even someone who would talk me out of this whole thing. Jay? Would he do? Nope. No way I'd trust the judgment of a guy who'd let Esther Lakewood wrap him around her finger. Then who? Luke? Maybe. While Jay untied the boat, I phoned him, but when he answered he told me he was in New York for a week. I wished him well.

It was two-thirty when we docked at Jay's place. I had five and one half hours before the meeting. Surely I could find someone by then? Telling Jay I'd think seriously about the offer, but probably wouldn't be able to decide until I got back to Cambridge, I headed back to my motel room. The workers were hard at work on the bridge. A familiar figure in a yellow hard hat sandwiched between Les and Zen walked toward me. Gator.

"Hey there, girl," he said, "you look like you ate something bad. Too many steamers?"

"Where'd you get that hat?"

He smiled. "Fished it out of the canal. Nice, huh?"

He tugged it down lower.

"Guess it'll keep you from getting beamed by a coconut."

Zen chuckled. "What's up?"

I looked at her and Les, then at Gator. Just maybe these Musketeers were my answer. Just maybe. "You ever hunt?"

Zen's grin broadened. "Are you kiddin'? We hunt the glades, hon. Best hunting country in Florida. Where do you think Gator got his name? We're hunting buddies. Right, Gator?"

Gator nodded, but was looking at me quizzically.

"Could we go to your office?" I asked him.

Sitting in front of the small grocery store, I took a deep breath and explained my dilemma. As I talked, I could see the wheels already churning in Gator and Zen's heads.

Gator spoke first. "Les, you'll stay here. Zen, you and I will go with this here gal."

Trust a man to take over. I would have to slow him down. I raised my voice and put my hands on my hips for emphasis. "Hey! This is my operation! I don't want it to look like I've brought a posse. Only one of you should come along."

But neither Gator nor Zen were listening. They were too caught up in the idea of having an official (well, whatever) capacity in a murder investigation. So what if it was being conducted by an artist. That didn't seem to faze them. Sighing, I leaned back in the chair and watched the traffic pass and let them work off their excitement. Already I felt safer. What could go wrong with this pair on my side?

When we parted, we had a plan. Gator and Zen would both accompany me to the sheriff's office, but I would let them out a block or so away and they would make it the rest of the way on foot. I returned to my room to pack and then take a needed, stress relieving, quality thinking, power walk.

21

*I've been absolutely terrified every moment of my life,
and I've never let it keep me from doing a single thing I wanted
to do.*

~Georgia O'Keeffe

I pulled into the parking lot of the sheriff's office at 7:00 p.m. on the dot. Gar was strapped in the passenger seat. I'd driven the last mile slowly, giving Gator and Zen plenty of time to position themselves in a nearby hiding place and to stay, unless they heard a signal for help. What signal? Zen had asked. A scream should do just fine, I told her.

Sheriff Marc Schilling's car was the only one visible. I'd hoped the dispatcher was working late. No such luck. Probably she was at the gym working out. I wished I was there, too— that is, if I liked gyms, which I didn't.

I'd already decided the meeting would be short. How long could it take for me to accuse the sheriff of murder and for him to try to off me? Yes, accuse him. By now, I was convinced he was the killer. Leaving Gar securely strapped in, I left my car, tapping the bill of my good luck cap with sweaty fingers.

"Hey!" The loud whisper sounded like wind hitting a tin roof. But there was no wind and the roof on the county building wasn't metal. Could Gator and Zen be any noisier? Not wanting to attract attention, casually I turned my head and saw Gator and Zen behind an oleander bush. I wondered if they knew the bush was poisonous. They waved. If they smiled, I'd seriously consider walking over and giving them a karate chop. Fortunately, they didn't.

I cleared my throat and acted as if I hadn't seen them. Sauntering, what I hoped seemed nonchalantly, I went toward the door.

"We've got your back, girl," Zen called out in another attention-getting whisper.

Ple…eese! Be quiet!

Swiping my sweaty palms on the back of my jeans and surprising myself, I sent up a prayer to help Zen keep her mouth shut, before opening the outer door. Hadn't I been the one in art school who proudly announced for all to hear that I didn't sweat or pray? Where had that girl gone?

The usually secured door leading to the sheriff's office was braced open. I went down the hall. His office overhead light was on. With the same eagerness I showed when I''d once been faced by a shark, I put my foot inside. Only twelve more feet to go. Stepping forward, I left the outer door open. Better to eat you, my dear, I thought.

"Sheriff?" I called out. I was beginning to feel even more nervous when no answer came back. "Sheriff?" A hint of scared made its way into my voice. I couldn't have been more thankful for the redneck who called herself Zen and the pirate-obsessed Gator, sidekicks who were surely inside by now.

I took two more steps. "Well, Sheriff, I guess you're not here. I'll call again tomorrow." More likely, I'd just call the cops in the next county, which I should have done in the first place. "Looks like we're going to have a storm tonight. Guess I'll be going. Bye now." A feeling, like I'd gotten when I received a letter from the IRS after April 15th, hit me with the force of a hammer. Pushing it away, I opened the office door and peeked inside.

The sheriff's high-backed chair faced the wall of photos

near the window. His muscular arm was slung over the right side with his fingers touching the floor. "Sheriff?"

Please don't let him be dead. Please.

Another step and I let out a squeak that bordered on a scream when the chair suddenly swiveled. Grabbing my chest, I laughed nervously, hoping Zen and Gator remained hidden. "Oh, Sheriff! You startled me. Why didn't you answer?"

A shuffling sound came from the hallway and I had to trust that the sheriff hadn't heard my back-ups backing up.

Why couldn't I just be home watching nighttime soaps? At times like this I hated the woman's movement and all that conscience-raising stuff.

"Siddown, my dear. I've been waitin` for you."

I stopped biting my lower lip only when my rump touched both sides of the seat of the padded chair. I kept my eyes on the floor. To distract the sheriff I crossed my legs and rocked my foot back and forth, but the ploy didn't work this time.

The sheriff's eyes drilled into mine. "Let me begin by saying that I admit when I first met you I thought you were a total ditz devoid of rational thought, someone without the DNA to be a decent P.I. and yet...here you are."

He tapped a cigar against his palm. "What am I going to do with you?"

I offered him a weak shrug. The sheriff gave me a "humph" and set the cigar near his phone. The simple action, for no reason I could think of, made me shiver—big time.

"Well, Ms. Murphy. We both know you broke into my office. That's a federal offense."

I straightened in my chair, ready to defend myself. "I did no such thing. The office wasn't locked."

He gave me an amused grimace. "Tell me what you're assuming. I'm fascinated." In silence, he added "bitch."

I slipped my hand in my jacket pocket and stealthily switched on the palm-sized tape recorder. Thank you, Hawk. Settling back into the chair, I crossed my legs and took a folded piece of paper out of my breast pocket. "See the photo on the wall behind you?"

He didn't bother to turn his head.

I unfolded the sketch and laid it on his desk. "Taco is your daughter, right? The same girl in that photo?"

"Hm. Can I keep this? Her mother would probably scrapbook it. Nice likeness." He put the sketch in his pocket. "So I guess in Boston, where you come from, it's a crime to be on the outs with your daughter?"

"Of course not." I squirmed. "Here's what I figure. I think Will, in his excitement of finding the treasure, told Taco about it and she mentioned it when you were around. And since, Sheriff, you're in possession of coins that came from that dig…"

His eyebrows arched. "You have proof of that?"

I blushed. Okay, I'd done it. I'd accused him. This is where he took out his pistol and aimed it at my heart. This is where my buds jumped in to save me. Prepared to be rescued like any damsel in distress, I swatted at the mosquito that whirled around my head.

Nonplussed Schilling picked up the unlit cigar and carefully balanced it on the ashtray, an action that was particularly irritating at this point.

But maybe the cigar was really a teeny, tiny gun. It was pointing at me. Was it time to scream? I opened my mouth as he began to talk.

"So the motive for the murder was greed?"

"Absolutely." I kept my eyes on the cigar.

"And you can prove I was at Rolins` apartment the night he was found?"

"I found a cigar butt. I plan to deliver it to the cops in the next county tomorrow." If I were still alive. He didn't need to know that I had lost that butt on the way home that very night. I can't find my keys half the time. I continued in a firm voice. "It has tooth prints that as we both know, are better than fingerprints." I'd seen that on a cop show. "Plus I have a feeling your fingerprints were all over Will's apartment. Of course, they'd be ignored because it would be assumed you were one of the first on the scene. But you weren't, Sheriff.

Were you? When that information is revealed I guess you'll have a lot of explaining to do." I was so proud of my rational conclusion that my voice had edge.

"A cigar butt? You're kidding, right?" He shrugged. "I was at that duplex a week before Will died. He had seen someone fooling with that sailboat out back and he called me. But I guess you wouldn't know that?"

I pursed my lips but did not meet his eyes.

"And, of course, I would know how to make a murder look like a suicide. I'm in the biz, right?"

I didn't like how the conversation was going. He was doing an excellent job of making my conclusion seem foolish and irrational—again.

Letting out a prolonged sigh, the sheriff leaned forward on his arms. His facial expression was kind. "Ms. Murphy, let me be specific. I asked you here to apologize. I had no intention of arresting you for the break-in of my office. Your tip concerning Rose Thompson helped us arrest dangerous terrorists who we discovered were planning another bombing at an abortion clinic. The people of Matlacha, of Florida, and in fact, of the U.S. will be forever in your debt."

Was the man who I had just accused of murder thanking me?

He continued. "You know, my dear, you've been fishing for a killer ever since you arrived here. And while I admire your persistence, have you come up with any hard evidence to prove your theory, or I should say, your hope that Will Rolins was murdered? The fact that I have old coins in my desk proves nothing. I'm a coin collector. The fact my daughter and I don't get along is none of your business.

"But, me a killer? Absolutely not. I understand that you want to eliminate your guilt. A man you loved had problems with depression and died fifteen hundred miles away. You feel responsible. That's natural. My dear, I really feel sorry for you. Anyone who has met you here feels sorry for you. But don't you think it's time to stop being so stubborn and admit the truth—Will Rolins killed himself."

He had hit a deeply vulnerable, tender spot. I *was* stubborn. I *did* feel guilt—every minute of each day.

Ten minutes later I was at the outer door feeling abashed.

The sheriff stood in the open doorway to his office. "Oh, and Ms. Murphy?"

"Yes?"

"Don't forget your two friends. They probably have dust on their knees. Our janitorial service isn't what it should be. Good night."

Great. Oh, just great.

I left feeling like a discarded breaded gherkin followed by Gator and Zen.

22

There is a logic of color, and it is with this alone, and not with
the logic of the brain, that the painter should conform.
~ Paul Cezanne

Later that night, after a super-sized power walk, I went
with Gar to the fish house and ate a mullet sandwich with fries
at the outside tables. Sipping a Guinness, I mulled over the
events of the past days. I felt defeated. The sheriff was right.
Irish, especially this one, were obstinate. I did have the wild
imagination of an artist. Why shouldn't I, I was an artist. I was
half Irish too. That didn't help. I did feel responsible for Will's
death. I had let him come down here on his own, knowing he
needed me to remind him to keep on his meds.

I took another bite of my crispy mullet and considered
what should come next. Acceptance. Facing reality. People did
kill themselves. Often the loved ones never knew why. "I
guess that's it," I said aloud.

"What's *it*?"

I jumped and beer sloshed over the sides of my plastic cup.
Mopping up the picnic table with a paper napkin that was
really a paper towel that my refined Grandma Murphy would
definitely not use—not in a trillion, billion years, I turned to

the woman standing behind me.

"So, you're finally admitting it?" Taco asked, raising a bottle of beer to her lips.

I shrugged. I really, really didn't want to talk to Taco or anyone else right now.

Taco's eyes locked with mine, and then her gaze quickly dropped. Turning away, she flicked the ashes of her cigarette onto the floor. "Now that you've accepted his suicide, you'll be able to move on. Happy travels." She turned away and then glanced over her shoulder with a sly smirk on her face. "He was one of the best lovers I've ever had." Abruptly, she hurried away, knocking over a garbage can that just missed hitting Gar's head.

I gasped. They were lovers? Will had been untrue to me? Oh my God. Oh my God. Grabbing Gar, I sped out for the door. But Taco was nowhere in sight. I felt as if I would vomit. Oh, Will…you didn't…you promised... I hurried to a dark corner, put my back to a wall, slid to the floor and broke out into sobs.

Red-eyed and wasted, I walked to the edge of the drawbridge where a pelican was preening itself on a piling. The bird eyed me and brought its wings close to its body then turned its beak toward the sea. A grounded sailboat listed to the right. The pelican raised its bill toward the sky. Brilliant sunrays split a cloud in two. The clouds were in the shape of two profiles—a man holding a metal detector and a woman in a cap. The pelican flew away. The cloud that really, really looked like Will and me vaporized. I was stunned and felt I'd been given a message. It was time to give up and go home. Knowing when to cash in the chips is what made for a smart gambler.

Head down, I went back to the motel and retrieved Will's letters. I walked to the dock and tossed them into the dark water, watching them disappear before re-entering the room.

An hour later my easel, paints and supplies leaned against the wall near the unlocked door. Gar, in red sunglasses, sat on the table under the window. It was foggy, but I planned to leave immediately. I was tired of making a fool of myself, of grasping at brittle plastic straws. I needed to go home and get used to Will never coming back, of Will having betrayed our love. I zipped up my bag.

The faintest of noises snapped my head around. I caught my breath. It was past eleven. "Who's there?" I called out in a nervous, "oh, dear" voice. I bit my tongue as fear gripped my stomach muscles. Great. Oh, great! I'd just let whoever was there know I was alone. Way to go. I set down the bag, not taking my attention from the door.

My eyes flew to my cell phone. It was near Gar on the table. The distance seemed a thousand miles away. Was it time to scream?

Another sound on the dock made me grit my teeth. Could I make it to the bathroom? Did that door even have a lock? Instinct told me that danger was near. Opening my mouth, I screamed. The door burst open and I stared at a gun. Pointing right then left, Zen, just like in the movies, entered the room.

I gasped in relief and amazement. "Zen. Girl, you scared me to death. Why didn't you answer me?"

"Answer you when?"

Apparently Zen hadn't heard me call out. Grabbing Gar I hugged him to me and collapsed onto the bed.

"You okay?" Zen asked, sliding the gun into her pant's pocket.

I pulled Gar even closer.

Zen stepped outside and assured the other motel guests and the manager that I had had a nightmare. She re-entered the room.

I pushed up from the bed. "You should have told me you'd be out there."

"Yeah, well…." She saw the bag and frowned. "You leavin`?"

"Yep."

"What about Will's killer?"

I spoke with conviction. "Will committed suicide. It's time to accept that." I headed for the door.

"So there's no mystery, no murder to solve?"

"No, there's no mystery, no murder, just a senseless death to mourn." I said the words, but I knew I didn't believe them. Will would not kill himself—no way. But someone else was going to have to take over. I was done. Done. Will, you jackass.

I hated goodbyes, so after loading the car, I told Zen I'd phone or write the others later, and then gave her a hug before settling behind the wheel. A mile down the road I switched on the radio then fingered Gar's ear, trying not to think of Taco and her dad and Will's death. What if the greedy Taco had killed Will and taken the chest? When Taco's dad arrived on the scene he found something in the apartment that proved Taco had been there, got rid of it and somehow convinced her to give up the chest? Was that reasonable? Yes it was. Would I regret not at least talking to Taco again? Was I going to let my disappointment in Will stop me from tying up all the threads of the investigation? Was I really that poor of an investigator? I ran my tongue around the inside of my mouth, and then glanced at Gar. His body color seemed more vivid. I looked into the sky. The moon was brighter than I'd ever seen it.

"Hang on!"

Slamming down on the gas pedal, I spun the steering wheel and twisted into a sharp U-turn. I glanced at my car clock: 11:58. I had a hunch I knew where Taco would be.

The parking area in front of Bert's was filled, so I veered into the graveled lot of Bert's Pine Bay Art Gallery across the street and found a spot facing the pass. Through heavy fog I could see the silhouettes of fishermen and women lining the bridge. "Gar, you stay put. Don't worry, I'll be cautious," I said, before sliding the tape recorder into my pocket and leaving the car.

I was glad I was wearing a white shirt. It made crossing the busy road less hazardous. Drivers were supposed to give pedestrians the right of way at the crosswalk, but I never trusted they would. I stepped forward and put up my right arm so the pickup heading my way would stop. It didn't. I shook my fist and stepped forward. The oncoming car slowed, and then stopped. I waved my thanks and hurried across the road before I could be clipped from the other side.

When I opened the front door to Bert's the usual din assaulted my ears. Either the place was getting smaller or my ears were getting more sensitive. I took in the room, spotting Taco sitting on a bar seat talking to a woman I didn't know. It was apparently not Taco's night to work. Good. Easier to get her aside. I weaved around a pool stick extended behind a woman's back. Her black cowboy hat was pushed high on her head. I pulled my cap bill down. Sidestepping a couple who had their foreheads touching, I headed for the bar. A musician leaned against a stool strumming an electric guitar and singing country.

"Hey, Taco." I slid onto the seat to Taco's right.

She looked at me with raised eyebrows. "You still here?"

"Nice to see you too," I said, ordering a Guinness from a waitress I didn't recognize. Lil was not in sight.

"Just thought you were gone, that's all," Taco mumbled.

I rubbed my neck muscles. "Will be soon. Plan to be skirting Orlando in a few hours."

Taco's expression became friendlier. She introduced me to the woman on her left and she shared a joke. I chuckled, biding my time. The stranger slid off her stool and said her farewells.

Bert's was not the place to accuse Taco. But, as of now, I hadn't figured out where the best place would be. Fortunately, Taco provided the answer.

"Well, see you. I need a smoke," Taco said, standing. "Drive safe."

Taco hadn't paid, so she would return. I knew that the workers at Bert's were in the habit of smoking out by the dumpsters in front of the building that was used for storage space for Bert's. I let Taco pass through the door before I dropped three dollars on the bar. My plan did not include a return.

Taco leaned against a dumpster inches away from the remains of a discarded anchor and two well-used white five-gallon buckles, cigarette in hand. I hesitated. I hated all things dumpster. The germs. The flies. The rancid smells. What would Grandma Murphy think? Cringing, I straightened my shoulders, stuck my fingers in my pocket, switched on the mini tape recorder and walked directly to her.

"You stalkin` me?" Taco blew smoke into the air.

I folded my arms in front of me, kind of like my mom used to do when she was projecting "serious". "Nah. Just wanted to ask you a couple questions and didn't want to do it inside."

Taco nodded at a biker as he entered Bert's. "Questions? About what?" She stepped backward until she was hidden by the shadows of an eight-foot fence and the two-story house used for storage. I followed her and was surprised with how isolated we were.

"Like, why didn't you tell me you were the sheriff's daughter? Why keep it a secret?"

Taco sniffed and tossed her cigarette butt. "What difference would it make to you?"

Realizing I was breaking Hawk's core rule of not facing a suspected killer alone with my suspicions, I took a step toward Taco. "Well, actually, quite a lot. Once I realized you were the sheriff's daughter and neither of you were sharing that information with me, I was able to put two and two together. This is how I see it. When Will told you that he was planning to give the treasure to the historical society, you couldn't handle it and killed him. Your dad realized that you did it and covered up for you." Okay. Okay. I have a big mouth and have been accused of speaking without using my reasoning facilities more than once. Sorry Grandma.

Taco's face was no longer the face of a beautiful young woman, it was pure angered monkey. Her fists clenched. Her jaw tightened. I glanced around. Dark. Isolated. Scary. Shit. But I could scream, I told myself. Taco's voice lowered to a whisper. "There's no witness to this conversation. It would be your word against mind, so I'll tell you. I guess you have a right to know what happened. It was Will's fault. He shouldn't have made me mad. Christ, you're right. He was going to give up all that gold! I couldn't believe it. The gun was on his desk. When I picked it up, he tried to take it from me and it went off. I'm really sorry that he died. He was a nice guy. He just shouldn't have had the gun around."

My blood felt like it had turned to a juicy Slurpee. "You killed him? *You* killed Will?" I really hadn't expected this.

Taco recoiled. "I thought you said you knew."

"You bitch! How would I have known that? It was conjecture on my part. You *killed* him?" I lunged at her. "You bitch!"

Taco grabbed my arm, twisted it behind my back and dragged me farther away from Bert's. Her other hand covered my mouth as I struggled. Fire shot through my arm. I tried to open my mouth to bite her, but her grip was too strong. I wiggled this way and that. Taco held tight.

"You want to know the rest before I snap your neck?" Taco's hissed in my ear. "It was my dad who took the treasure to the historic society. When he showed up at Will's apartment he found my jacket and realized I'd been there. He convinced me I was stupid to think I could sell the contents of the chest and get away with it. He sent it to some lousy historic place or other. I shouldn't have listened to him. I could be in South America by now. He doesn't know everything."

I broke free. "I guess he knows you killed Will, you greedy witch."

"Why, you..." Swiftly Taco's arm shot out, grabbed a rusty piece of anchor and caught me in the arm. With a loud grunt, I went down on one knee. Taco pulled her leg back and slammed her shoe into my gut. I groaned and could no longer focus, but struggled to stand. Taco raised the anchor again. Hearing the whoosh, woozy and fighting for my life, I whirled, snapped my leg up and slammed it against Taco's forearm. The anchor flew high in the air, landing in the water with a loud splash. With another expert karate maneuver I spun again, and with one arm to Taco's gut, dropped her to the ground, collapsing beside her.

Massaging my other arm I watched a pelican swoop low

and head straight for us. Then splat! The bird did a number on Taco's beautiful, brunette hair.

Poor Taco. How was she going to face a camera looking like that?

23

I decided that if I could paint that flower in a huge scale, you could not ignore its beauty.
~ Georgia O'Keeffe

After Taco and her dad were arrested, I was instructed by the police chief deputy of Collier County to remain in the area until no further questioning was necessary. It was confirmed the coin I'd taken for authentication had come from Will's treasure. Detectives had played my tapes to both Sheriff Schilling and Taco. Signed confessions were filed immediately. Hawk's son was home from the hospital and doing surprisingly well. Relieved, vindicated, but still grieving, I checked back into the motel, and it didn't take long for Luke to come knocking at my door with an idea.

Brush in hand, with three gallons of paint near my feet; I stood near an aluminum stepladder under the shade of the north side of Luke's gallery. Gar was sitting on a turquoise chair, watching behind his red sunglasses. Luke was leaning against a palm tree, ice cream cone in hand. His head was back dropped by a cloudless azure blue sky. Zen was sitting in the giant rocker across the street preparing to take another lick from her melting coconut frozen delight. She wore jeans and an oversized white shirt. Lil, in red short shorts and a black T-shirt, was setting on a red bench beside Zen. Both women had on floppy straw hats. Cars and trucks whizzed past. Tourists walked in and out of shops. A white egret stood near Lil. The air smelled of dead fish. Not far away, Jay and Gator were in serious conversation.

"Are you sure you should be climbing that thing?" Luke asked.

I laughed. "If you can't watch me, go inside. Remember, this was your idea. Did I fall yesterday or the day before?"

Luke took another lick. "No. And you bet it was my idea and a darn good one. I need to get something inside, but then I'm standing right here to catch you if you fall." He rushed around the corner.

Clutching a paint pot and placing three brushes into the pocket of my painter's pants, I climbed. My flip flops grabbed the rungs just fine. I smiled and began to whistle a low tune.

Two men carrying fishing poles and yellow bait buckets walked by and waved gaily.

Grinning, while taking another step, I raised my brushes to wave, then "Ohhhh!" Down I went. Thump. Thump. Thump. All the way to the bot...tom. Plop! Paint splashing. Brushes flying.

Checking for possible broken bones and finding none, I swiped my nose with the back of my hand and looked up into Zen's concerned eyes. "You okay, hon?"

"Yeah, sure. No broken bones. Just embarrassed."

Next Luke, Gator, Jay and Lil came into focus.

"Don't stand."

"You really, really shouldn't wear flip flops when climbing a ladder," Lil said as Luke began to pick up my scattered brushes and I bent to right my paint pot.

"Sorry about the mess," I said to Luke.

"You're okay. That's the important thing."

Zen's hands were behind her back.

They shook their heads in amusement as I planted my now painted feet—anyone can have painted toenails--on level ground and felt my butt again. A bruise most likely, but nothing more serious. Zen's eyes twinkled. So did the others. "So, what's up?"

Zen giggled. "Wipe that paint off your hands and close your eyes."

"What?" I sent a puzzled look in Luke's direction.

He winked.

"Come on, you stubborn northerner, close your eyes," Lil said.

Shaking my head, I did as I was told.

"Now, hold out your hands."

I wrapped my fingers around an object that fit easily within my palm.

"Okay. Open them!" Zen said.

"Oh, a manatee!"

Putting my thumb and forefinger on the pink ribbon attached to the head of the small figure, I gazed at the giant half-finished pelican on the side of Luke's gallery and wiggled the gift. "Look, she's wearing flip flops!"

Zen clapped her hands. Gator pulled out another cigarette. Scratching her head above her right ear, Lil shuffled her feet. Jay bent and scooped up Gar.

"It's something to take with you to remind you to come back," Zen said.

A breeze blew across the pass, making the water tickle the shore.

ABOUT THE AUTHOR

jd daniels` prize-winning fiction and poetry has appeared in various publications, including: *The Broad River Review, The Sylvan Echo, The Elkhorn Review* and *Doorknobs & Body Paint Fantastic Flash Fiction: An Anthology.* She received a prize for poetry from Emerson College/Cambridge University, is listed in the Iowa Arts Council and Poets & Writers Directories and is an active member of PEN Women of Southwest Florida. Her book, *The Old Wolf Lady: A Biography* was published in 2005 by a grant from The Boston Arts Council. She was awarded her Doctor of Arts degree from Drake University for her collection of poems, *Currents That Puncture* and is co-founder and an editor of *Prairie Wolf Press Review.* Her book of poetry *Say Yes* placed her Number One on the Cedar Rapids Gazette bestseller list. Besides following her passion, she enjoys kayaking, playing tennis, bicycling, walking and laughing with her friends and family.

She has a website and would love to hear from you:

http:live-from-jd.com

OTHER BOOKS BY THE AUTHOR

FICTION

Minute of Darkness

NON-FICTION

The Old Wolf Lady: A Biography
(First Edition)

The Old Wolf Lady: Mawewa Mepemoa
(Second Edition)

POETRY

Currents That Puncture: A Dissertation

Say Yes

Made in the USA
Middletown, DE
12 February 2017